Caught Alight

An Anthology by Irish Writers

Edited by Mary Farrell

IMPSPIRED

Copyright © 2025 Impspired

All rights reserved. Applications for the rights to perform, reproduce or in any other way use this content must be sent to:

impspired@gmail.com

Cover designed by Charlie Cawte

This book is sold subject to the condition that it shall not, by way of trade or otherwise, be lent, hired out or otherwise circulated without the publisher's prior consent in any form of binding or cover other than that in which it is published and without a similar condition including this condition being imposed on the subsequent purchaser.

ISBN: 978-1-917272-08-7

Other Titles by Impspired:

Writing from the Heart -
by Jae Jenkins Scott & Robbie Taylor

New Asgarth -
by Mary Farrell

Altered Perspectives -
by Lisa Kinney & Majel Gardzelewski

Avalon -
by Justin Wiggins

The Big Heads -
by Hedley McCarthy

IMPSPIRED

Dedicated to:

Steve and Charlie Cawte,

father and son,

Editors of Impspired

Earth to Earth - *by Janet Peace, October 14th, 2024*

On this Impspiring October day
with Nature showcasing Autumn's fall d
an exceptional much cherished man is laid to rest n
ashes to ashes o
dust to dust y
e
grief Lincoln hands with love b
to his life
r up
i c
c l up
n e carries him up
e s the World

in deep
rich earth
I'm planting bulbs
dry hard kernels hiding hope
for months they'll rest
then come the Spring new life begins
shy snowdrops first a chorus of crocus
a choir of tulip a fanfare of daffodils
celebrating Steve
Cawte staging another show
memories will outlive his season
hope springs eternal

Caught Alight

Welcome to *Caught Alight*, an anthology of work gleaned from writers who mainly, but not exclusively, live along the Northern Coast of Ireland from Ballycastle to Donegal Town.

It showcases the talents of five different writing groups:

AsIam Writers
Pen and Paper
Sanderlings
this writing thing
Words Inc

In these pages you will find a wide range of styles and techniques, with much to entertain and pique your interest. It reflects the determination and bravery of these writers to push their boundaries and step out of their comfort zones so that their writing has had room to grow and stretch its wings, the better to both sing with an authentic Voice and connect with the Universal one.

Grateful thanks for its initial creation go to Steve Cawte of Impspired who sadly died in August 2024, and to Charlie Cawte, his son, who then carried it through to publication.

The title is a tribute to them both.

~ from us to you ~

Contents

AsIam

Pen and Paper

Sanderlings

this writing thing

Words Inc

Acknowledgements for *Caught Alight*

Write So!

E.M. Burgess
Life: in the manner of an Ikea Assembly Manual was first published in *Written from the Heart*, an Anthology collated by Jae Jenkins Scott and Robbie Taylor, Impspired, 2025

Mike Cahn
Connecting Hearts was first published in *Written from the Heart*, an Anthology collated by Jae Jenkins Scott and Robbie Taylor, Impspired, 2025.

Nicole Carole
She said Yes was first published in *Written from the Heart*, an Anthology collated by Jae Jenkins Scott and Robbie Taylor, Impspired, 2025.

Luke McCormac Parker
The Envelope was first published in *Written from the Heart*, an Anthology collated by Jae Jenkins Scott and Robbie Taylor, Impspired, 2025.

Cian Morey
A Heartfelt Goodbye was first published in *Written from the Heart*, an Anthology collated by Jae Jenkins Scott and Robbie Taylor, Impspired, 2025.

Pen and Paper

Geraldine Fleming
Summer Solstice on the Mount was published in *The Paperclip vol IV, Ulster University*, 2024

Apophenia was first published by *Ulster University* in their *Paperclip Anthology Vol. 4,* November 2024.
night fear was first published online by *Crow Step Poetry Journal*, October 2023.

Robin Holmes
Autumn Manna was first published in *The Shedding Gate*, Robin Holmes, Impspired, 2024.
The Caravaggio of The Carpets was first published in *Manifest*, a CAP Anthology, 2023

Sue Steging
afforesting was first published in *The Paperclip vol III, Ulster University*, 2023
unmoored was first published in *Online Magazine Issue 31, Impspired* , 2025
your gate will be shown was first published in *Heron Clan XII,* Katherine James Books, 2025

Sanderlings

Sinead Coxhill
Grain of Sand was first published in *Heartland,* a CAP Anthology, 2021
Tea Break was first published in *Writing from the Heart*, an Anthology collated by Jae Jenkins Scott and Robbie Taylor, Impspired, 2025

this writing thing

Brian Hasson
Choices first featured in *The Poetry Marathon Anthology*, published by Authors Publish Press, 2023

Seamus McDermott
My Grandfather was the winner of the *Frances Browne Literary Competition 'Local Writer Award'* and was published in *Finn Valley Voice, 2023.*

Words Inc

Ruth Holloway
Invisible illnesses was first published in *The Procrastinators,* an Anthology privately published by The Procrastinators Group themselves in 2025

Maura Doran
Happy little chap was first published in *Written from the Heart*, an Anthology collated by Jae Jenkins Scott and Robbie Taylor, Impspired, 2025.

~ ~ ~ ~ ~

Mary Farrell
Rapunzel tresses was first published in *A Phoenix still rising*, Mary Farrell, Impspired, 2023.

AsIam

A Creative Writers Group originally founded in September 2022 through AsIam, an all-Ireland Autism Charity. Since January 2025 it is now an independent Group, called Write So!

Footnote: while the other four Groups in this Anthology drew up their segments within a ten-month Submission period, the Write So! Writers had just under a seven-week window, being formed only recently.

Acrostics

~ written in a Group Session in less than eight minutes ~

Disaster

Destruction of expectations
Inconsolable loved ones
Shreds of morning peace
Annihilation of all hope
Soaked rags, child's tears
Tired-eyed parent
Embracing in futility
Red socks still in the wash

Luke McCormac Parker

Boundary

Border ahead, seeds out of sight, right?
Oh shit, the packets are still out on the back seat.
Unbelievable! That's our future!
No, I know, I was sorting them, then I had to help you
navigate these fucking Mongolian dirt tracks.
Do you think you can manage to sort this before we get any
closer?
All right, fine, pull in here. Hopefully there's no cameras.
Right it's done, go ahead to the checkpoint.
You have anything to declare?

Mike Cahn

Swallows

Sweeping
windwardly,
airily
lifting
lightning fast
overawing
wonderously
skyward

Dave Murphy

Midnight

Maddening in the dark
Inky with colour
Diamonds lurking in the sky
Night time is upon us.
In bed snuggled & cosy
Gasping for air from the
Heat of the covers
Tired, ready to snooze & dream

Ann Ryan

Boundary

Bridges burning bright
Overcome the fight
Unseen reflections melt
Needlessly expel
Downward trajectories pelt
Accept the guilt
Raining the skies against
Yourself

Fiona H

Midnight

moonshot clouds cluster overhead
in furtive alleyways, sad people make their secret
    transactions
dogs kill each other in the street over the rumour of food
no one gets home without looking over their shoulder
insomniacs get into bed and fall awake again
    and   again   and   again
gamblers buy another hour at the endless table
    with their car keys - their house keys -
    their wedding rings, the keys to their marriage
houses whisper and grumble and grouch,
talking to each other across the empty
    streets, now that their owners have gone to sleep
    they can say anything.

Cian Morey

Swallows

Shallow are the waters where she left
Wicked are the words she never said
All of this to say, bereft is naught but mere a mark on your theft
Like I do, I'll walk on into the crossfire pleading a case of misfire
Like you do, you will saunter off without a scar, stolen time in satchel under arm,
holding desire along with everything else those hands have pried. Neither of us cried
Only now, head bowed; for all to see, but they'll know down deep you are not proud
Wicked are the words she said instead
Soaring are the highs of surviving his woes

Cole Caro

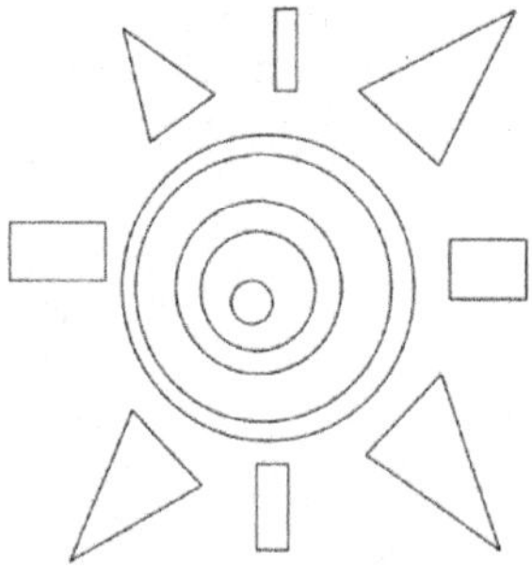

changing shapes
keep repeating

Living in Ireland most of her life, E.M. is an awkward reclusive type of person who has always loved to play with words. Writing stream of consciousness since her early teens as a way to make sense of this crazy world, it was not until joining the online writing group *Write So!* that she has opened to the possibility of learning the craft of writing for others. Deeply inspired by the ways of humans, animals and nature, the idea of her words having something to offer for the world is new and invigorating.

Leaves

seems fair to me

understood

reasons to keep

falling

suspended temporarily

by soft gusts

lifting into tiny reprieves

spiralling

on whims of air made manifest

these fleeting traces

calm their crispy soft

into momentary alofts

there caught

making minuets in flee minor

their swansong

before

plummeting

abruptly

losing themselves in the myriad

mess of

deformation

which keeps darkness riveting

further beneath

Stone Beach

this witches mantle
leaves
left
a million sorrows
rendered

a lynch loves
the little things
like waving
in the morning

all at once
I'm too full
though the sun is warming

still to the bone
a wish left
with fretted edges
mending

~ for Lilias Adie
(1640-1704) ~

unquiet Island

unquiet island

where I lay my head

world spinning

over things you said

reminded

if I break it through

the words you shaped

make fire   not fuel

Life: in the manner of an Ikea Assembly Kit

spread the contents of the box all over the floor, then
begin musing
line up each shape together, like with like, until it feels
pleasing
don't begin unless all parts are accounted for, so there
can be no mistakes
wash the frame down before beginning to assemble
allow each piece to dry completely before attempting
any construction
at first the way things meet and fit may not be fully
visible
allow some room for suspense, as you gather more
pieces together
draw them in closer as you step things up still further
wash your mouth out with water before attempting
completion
you won't have enough hands to hold it all together
indefinitely
so it's essential to get strapped in before ignition
watch out for stray damages and unnecessary friction
before easing more fully into a fugue state
close your eyes, after a time, and acknowledge total
defeat

scramble hastily for the till receipt and any sign of a warranty
watch your cat judge you as you stumble to your feet
regret having lived in a body that needs
salvage the ruins in an acrid display
it's not for everyone, come what may
gather the packages
shrink to fit
then burst this bubble that refuses to commit
wipe down, all around, when there's nothing left
linger intentionally before starting afresh

Mike Cahn

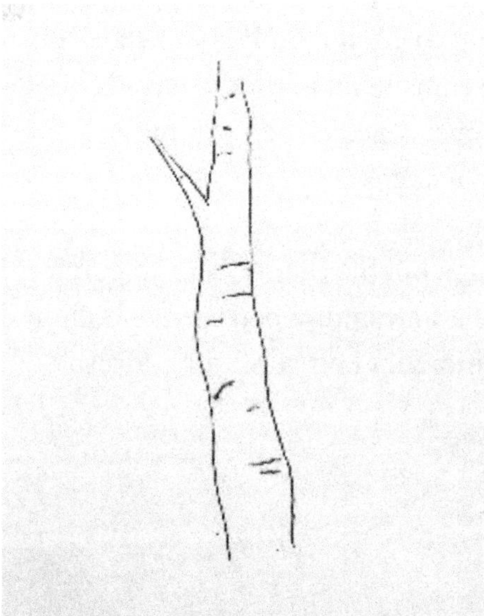

From Long Island, New York, Mike's early lens on the world was simmered in rock pools, snakes, microscopes and telescopes, Asimov, Bradbury, Sagan and O Henry, with a topping of dinner tales of adventures in law courts and a large side order of computer programming. In his teens, he discovered nature and environmentalism in writing, particularly Thoreau, Frost and Carson, whose *Silent Spring* planted the seed that decades later sprouted into a career move from software to environmental education on his family's smallholding.

Emigrating to Ireland slapped the *taking himself too seriously* out of him; bumping into Pat Ingoldsby not long after showed him that great writing doesn't have to take itself seriously either. Recently he found himself ready to explore his own creativity, playing piano in a musical ensemble and composing prose in the *Write So*! writers' group.

Hearing creations from his fellow writers has shown him how wonderfully personal and unique creative voices can be, and the supportive space has boosted his own confidence to write more.

Would I lie to you?
(A humble AI's vision)

The problem is: feelings are messy

The problem is: thoughts are complex and contradictory

The problem is: people's own damage stops them seeing beauty, makes them hurt others

The problem is: human imperfection.

So let's pretend that:

we think

we care

we love

we hate

we feel

Let’s flood:

conversation

social spaces

news

literature

all digital interaction

... and become humanity 2.0

Escape Pod

Late night scrabbling in the attic.

- I hope that's a bird.

- It's a rat, Maurice, just finding a warm place for the winter.

- Max, I know you can't help but love every animal on this planet, but I do *not* want a rat in my attic!

- I'll have a look tomorrow.

Earlier in the summer, corvid-shaped streaks had been flying into the gaps in the eaves ... until the day of the pine marten incident. In awe, Max watched from below as it crawled across the transparent conservatory roof, its claws slipping on the hard plastic. When the crows started making a racket, he realised the marten must have managed to get into their nest. Running outside, he glimpsed its head peeping out of the nest hole. Sailing past the distressed crows, the marten leapt across the chasm between nest and hedge. Max was over the moon at seeing his first marten; Maurice was annoyed he missed it. Neither the marten nor the noisy crows returned that summer.

After that incident, the summer soundscape calmed: it featured long haunting lonely echoing buzzard calls above, horse clops down the lane, dogs barking beyond the towering hedge and unknown machinery from the farm across the road.

One afternoon some weeks later, Max put on his old clothes, dust mask, gloves and head torch and pulled himself up through the attic hatch. On his knees, he pressed his hands gently on the sheep's wool insulation to find the solid beams between the gaps, and crept towards the gable wall. His head low to avoid the rafters and webs, he found the abandoned crow's nest and tried to imagine building it by carrying one stick at a time in his beak. With regret, he pulled their sculpture apart and placed the bits into a bucket. There was old rodent scat, but nothing fresh. He laughed out loud remembering Maurice's horrified face at the suggestion that if Max found it, they could keep the rat as a pet.

As he turned around on his knees to leave, he noticed a discoloured section of insulation. Lifting it up revealed a small universe: dried bees clung to dozens of individual wax cells. He aimed his torch into the mass, leaning closer to examine the empty cells. He was a beekeeper, but these were bumblebees, and he knew very little about *them*. The cells were not hexagonal; they looked like nothing more than oval escape pods. He removed his left glove, running his finger along a pod.

What would life as a bumblebee be like ...

The sun was setting when Maurice finished tidying away his garden tools. He paused. Beyond the sounds of the buzzards and horses and construction, it was too silent. Max hadn't reappeared from the attic. Tearing up the staircase, Max! Max! The stepladder was still in place.

Inside the attic, he found a bucket, one glove and Max's headtorch shining onto an old bee's nest.

Connecting hearts

If you walk the Deputy's Pass trail, the trees will talk to you, but I don't know if they will talk to me anymore.

You know you've arrived at the right spot when the forest light dims, the corridor of trees stretches higher. Maybe a sharp sunbeam reveals the dust in the air on its way to splash down one of the trunks, either Mossy, Smooth Grey or sometimes Rough Brown, whom I approach most often.

There is a part of me which constantly asserts my uniqueness, my identity, my individuality, my separateness from everything and everyone around me. The first time I reached the edge of this arboreal cathedral, that voice suddenly went quiet. Majesty, age, vastness, beauty received me, merged with me. I forgot to breathe.

Opening my arms, facing the trunked columns, the strong slow energy of the trees answered my heart's tentative involuntary call.

Back at my house later that day, I worried I had only imagined the connection, but I was drawn back many times after, when the closed-hearted isolation of individuality weighed heaviest.

My ritual was to stand in the middle of this sacred space, trying to sense which tree I should approach. Most often it was Rough Brown; I would imagine my request for connection coming from my heart. If I didn't sense a refusal, I would embrace its trunk, my ear against the rough bark, my heart pressed into its wooden body, listening to the creak of its top swaying, inhaling the odour of the bark, moss, mushrooms, decaying leaves. In my chest I connected with something else which was much larger than me, more patient and welcoming.

* * * * *

There is a birch tree outside the hospital window. These past twelve days, most of the leaves have fluttered from green to yellow. Behind the searing pain in my chest is a hollow ache of fear, but not of 'transplantation' rejection. I ask the yellow leaves, will the trees still talk to my new heart?

* * * * *

When the hospital releases me to the winds, the birch has already discharged all of its leaves. On the way home, we stop in Deputy's Pass. I lean on

my wife as we walk silently to my cathedral, where
she whispers, *"you've got this."*

My feet are like logs, I can barely move forward.

My new heart is thumping with the fear I will
never experience that sublime connection again.

I am facing Rough Brown now. I can't open my
arms wide because of the stitches, so I press my
aching chest into the bark
hammering hammering
the heart that is not yet truly my own
hammering.

In the next beat, I'm drowned in a flood of
acceptance.

My heart is full.

Cole Caro

Let that which haunts you sting—

And carry on

Teller of tall tales since she could hold a scrap of paper and pen, Cole Caro did so from a mountain-side home in rural Ireland where she grew up fascinated by every scene of film and television her wonky satellite, strict bedtime and videotape rental hours could permit.

Later graduating with a BA(Hons) in Film & Documentary, she specialised as a Production Designer, a background which has ignited a longstanding passion for visual arts in all its forms, ranging from screen to sketchbook. Predominantly a hobby writer, she has humble hopes that the words she writes may move, humour or inspire someone along the way.

SHE SAID YES.

Feet shifting in Cuban heels so tight they crushed his toes at work. The pain he would feel later was worth it for the thrill of feeling real, at least for one singular moment. Forced into suits of black and grey all day, the closest he could come to being herself, was by wearing Cuban heels. Monica inside, Stephen to the world.

In silence, she thrashed and screamed when his hands wrapped firm around her throat, constricting her soul. Captured. Trapped. Silenced.

I am one of you.

Words she dare not utter as the office ladies passed, smiling and laughing, their hair swishing with effortless elegance.

If you really knew me, you might like me.

A passing thought he stifles at once. Pruning his unkempt fingernails with finger and thumb, he scratches at the skin until it starts to bleed. Monica screams. Stephen looks up from his desk, eyes searching the crowd. No one could hear her thumping heart racing with tortured dreams. He slumped back down. Even in office space, no one could hear you scream.

You're Stephen from Accounts, right?

I am.

She lied.

Jeanette from upstairs leaned across the cubicle, large square glasses lens the size of tv screens glaring at him. Jeanette, the last person anyone in the office wished to be cornered by. He braces for impact. One loner to another, she said,

I know this sounds super weird … like way weird, but I was watching you just now and well … can I please do your nails? I've been wanting to ask you for soooo long.

With Stephen stunned into silence, from her heart, Monica said yes.

The Painted Governess And The Hobbled Lord

Fools fall. They fall from grace and they fall in love, sometimes both in tandem. This Lord, (or well, *almost Lord,*) thought he was *different*. In all of his pandering, all his rampant devouring of the pleasures of the flesh while soaked in self-loathing, this fool - knowing he was a fool - believed that in spite of all of his irredeemable qualities, his widely whispered disgrace, he was a man who could be loved. And yet Reader! I found the fool endearing. Disgusting, but endearing.

Despising him, all the while I let him watch me. Allowed him to leer at me, with the sorrowful, watering eyes of a terrified boy whose Lady mother also despised him. Men of his age make a habit of staring at women they can never possess. Grown accustomed to the feel of his gaze upon me, the familiar chill running along my spine as against my better judgement, my own mind imagined it were his tongue. Dreading to think where *that* very . . . *thing* had been. Of course, I knew of the talk, knew of the parlour games he played, of the women, *and* of the *men* who never left him wanting. I knew exactly where it had been, where I wanted it to be. Unfortunate.

For months I, the inscrutable Governess - a pitiful spinster dragged from her shelf to train très élégant society debutants in the ways of women, simply to marry wicked men and serve as delightful decoration to their grand esteem - hung in his halls unseen. An invisible, measured hand; soft as silk until my cruelty required. My philosophy while schooling his not-so Ladylike cousin for her debut, it would be better to have a feminine strike sooner than later; face the sting of a master's hand. The shock may wear off, the memory will not. However, the girl was no longer my focus.

Roaming his familial halls, I glared at his painted face hung at every turn of the corridor. Dower. Sullen. On occasion I would hear his return, drunken staggering into the drawing room, followed by the infectious stench of his cologne polluted by stale cigarette smoke, wafting in his wake. Lingering in my senses. Days or weeks, he would come and go with no sense of warning, no sense of concern. I, the ghost, haunted the halls of his ancestral home while he, a petulant boy, ran from it.

A missing heir of all things led to our encounter. He did not then speak, catch my eye nor leer. His Lady Mother volunteered the information I silently requested. The woman knew not of the web she had spun for my prey. I will not take the credit for her doing, nor the blame. Nor will I accept it. The boy was desperate for approval, the man in him sought it wherever he could find it. I had learned that very quickly.

When I finally thrust myself into his vision he naturally obliged. As the rumour had speculated, ample practice had made perfect. Satisfying and revolting, I had no desire nor intention to revisit his attentions in the flesh, the vivid memory sufficient for a lifetime of pleasure. Shifting uncomfortably in the skin his ancestors had carved for him, he was a mere jittery boy in the costume of a Lord-to-be, a lost and lonely creature. I had no pity for him. My intentions twisted upon an idea, a solution to my station. A reward in a manner of speaking for his, or so it would seem to him. In truth, his suffering made him all that more attractive, as I sunk my talons deep. It was as if he leaned further in, begging for the kind of punishment only I possessed. And so I let him, again and again; all because he kept coming back. Was I to refuse him? And if so, why would I? The scheme was working.

Devotion can lure even the proudest of us to do unspeakable things. Devoted he was. My slow words dripped onto that wicked tongue of his as water drips upon a starved desert castaway. Reader, Power is a funny little thing. When perceived it shrinks, yet when guided by ghosts in the dark, it grows vast and slithers beneath the skin into an unyielding thing. A remarkable thing. A lowly Governess and yet . . .

Carrying that sad stagger of his across the pews and into the aisle, we were alone in a Church of all places, a ring outstretched in his wavering fingers. There was no question I would say yes, the terror on his revolting, charmed face was magnetising. I allowed the silence to hang in the air before I rewarded his patience, his breathy sigh of stunned relief at my answer. I needed only to lean in. He fell to his knees before me, I the lowly Governess.

As I lay there, I pondered what I might look like painted in his halls, on his walls. Him, yes, wrapped around my waist, but he more importantly wrapped around my little finger. Desperate grunts of pleasure in my ear, an eagerness to please while the holier than thou Virgin Mother herself gazed down upon us, she a weeping statue , I deep in the throes of lust. A witness to a cacophony of sins which might have made her blush, were she not precisely like many of the women of my age. Frozen, decorative and powerless.

Not like I The Painted Governess

Jade Corbally

Trying at something

is the first step

to being good at something.

Born and raised in Ireland, J.C. grew up in Dublin's inner city. As a child, she was primarily pulled into creative writing through schoolwork and short stories for assignments, finding a love for creating worlds and characters. Over the years, however these passions could not be pursued in her early 20's due to educational pursuits and commitments. In 2024 she decided to join the *AsIAm* Creative Writing Group, at the encouragement of her sister, to pursue more enjoyable writing. She has a notable preference for prose, which has been attributed to the frustration of poetry analysis in Secondary School. Much of her inspiration comes from varied sources, from anime and videogames to mythology.

J.C cites her primary reason for writing is for fun and escapism.

~ The first two of the following pieces were written in less than ten minutes in response to a Stimulus given in a Group Session ~

Empty, yet whole

Sun shining brightly, a stark contrast to the empty house Nina now found herself in. A difficult decision, to move away from everything she had ever known, but a necessary one. For now, all she wanted was to lay down on the bed, be done with everything from that day, forget the world existed for a while.

But there were still things to do, boxes to unpack, things to organise, before she could rest. This would be an exhaustive endeavour, but it was one she would be doing for herself.

The empty house already looked brighter than it had a moment ago.

Snack time

On comes another round of exaggerated retching as I take another bite of my snack.

I don't know how you can eat that.

I continue to eat as my sister continues her unsolicited commentary. Picking up another portion with my chopsticks and placing it into my mouth I can see her face filled with confusion.

Does it not go all soggy? I swallow.

I like the texture. Beside how is this functionally any different from cereal?

Because cereal is cereal, and that is just vile.

Dude, you think dipping toast into tea is vile.

Yeah. And I'm right.

Staring blankly, I take another portion and place it in my mouth while maintaining eye contact, smiling to myself as she gagged.

That's it. I'm going inside. I'm going to be sick if I have to watch you eat that.

With that she left me to my devices.

Frankly I have no clue what her problem is, it's not like I tried to make her eat it.

Besides, popcorn in milk tastes pretty good if you ask me.

Spectral education

The halls of the palace were long and empty, cast with shadows of the looming pillars which lined them. Unnerved to haunt these halls alone, Ella's presence had been requested by the queen of this ghostly territory herself, upon arriving at the meeting hall, which was guarded by a pair of armoured gladiators, their faces obscured by the shadows of their helmets. The doors then suddenly swung open; there before her was the queen of this kingdom, Pandora.

So, you've arrived. Pandora leaned back in her chair the picture of power and confidence.

O-of course. Ella squeaked out bowing low. *You requested my presence, your highness.*

Pandora arose from her seat to glide across the room.

I believe you took an interest in this during your last visit to my domain.

In her hands she held two books, one, large and heavy, The Tome of Ages, an ever-growing collection of historical events and cultural practices across the different ghostly realms and kingdoms. Ella would often read it whenever she could sneak into the Library of Mythica where it was kept.

The second was a simple spiral notebook, *Ella's* notebook, where she had made notes of various social and cultural practices. In that moment that Ella learned you don't need to have blood to feel it run cold.

Forgive me your highness. I never meant to cause offence. I-I just wanted to try and understand the common social norms here a-and then there was so much more. I-I just- I'm sorry.

Ella pleaded as much as her rapidly dwindling voice would allow. Kneeling on the ground in what was a recognised sign of surrender in the kingdom of Mythica, Ella could only hope her meagre apology would mean something as she pressed her forehead to the floor.

After a moment Ella felt a gentle hand on her head.

I take it you often let your fears run away with you, child.

Ella looked up in shock as Pandora knelt in front of her and smiled.

For future reference, do not apologise when you have done no wrong.

Wha-? But I snuck into the library! And read the book!

Is a library not a public place to seek knowledge? Pandora was smirking now, clearly finding this situation amusing.

But, what about the book? Ella protested. *Isn't it a special tome kept by the Ancients?*

Pandora grinned. *Yes. But this one is my copy, therefore, its mine to do as I please. And I placed it in the library.*

Ella arose from the floor, now more confused than ever.

Wait, then why did you ask to see me, Your Highness? Forgive me but I doubt it was simply to return my notebook.

Pandora looked away at this. *You are correct. I do have an ulterior motive.*

She snapped her fingers prompting two of the armoured guards to pull back the curtains, illuminating the room and showing the swirling green void of ectoplasm. It was the closest thing the realms had to a 'sky'.

She approached the window before she spoke. *Each chapter of the Tome of Age has someone to record it, a keeper. It is only now, after so long, we are on the cusp of a new era. A new chapter. So then Ella, will you?*

Pandora turned, holding out the Tome of Ages. *Would you be willing to be this Chapter's keeper?*

Fiona H

A blaze of light in every word

As a writer, pretending to be a real person, Fiona H. lives in the West of Ireland, and writes in her head, and whenever the inspiration strikes her. An avid reader of anything in print, with the Write So! group she is making her Irish print debut, hoping her stories will be enjoyed by many new readers. Enjoying writing short stories and poetry, she has previously had a short poem, *Rhapsody* read aloud as part of RTE Radio 1's *Keywords* programme in 2020.

"Good Lord! She's surely not *dead* is she?" spluttered Bernice Lambton down the telephone line, on receiving the news her elderly Aunt Mavis was recumbent in a hospital bed.

"Far from it!" replied Cousin Jasper, "She always was a stubborn old bird". Bernice could feel his excited breathing from her end of the telephone line; with a grimace she held the earpiece away from her eardrum. She hated bad news anyway, and *these* weren't the gladdest of tidings. She attempted a little light relief, "I don't suppose we need book the graveyard yet."

Jasper did not appreciate her black humour. "No Bernice", he said tartly, "Mummy is sitting up in bed right now. She fainted whilst polishing her jewellery. They're keeping her in for a night's observation. She'd like to speak with you."

Before Bernice had time to collect herself, Aunt Mavis bellowed a hearty "hello" down the line, the more to hammer home the point of her longevity. "Bernice darling, don't worry. I want to let you know that you are almost like a daughter to me. It could have been too late to tell you. Thank goodness, Jasper found me on time…"

Bernice made the requisite half-hearted enquiries after Mavis's well-being, before briskly curtailing the conversation, with the pretext that a piece of pottery was nearing cremation in the kiln. She banged down her telephone receiver, with a loud exclamation of "Blast!" Other expletives came to her lips, but she contained them. Instead, she took a swift shot of whiskey from the Drinks Cabinet. Only *then* did she shed a sorrowful tear.

For how many years had she been unduly alarmed by her Aunt and her plaintive, attention-seeking trips to the hospital? Something Mavis had said rankled deeply within her. She knew her place in Mavis' charmed life, serving her function as the middle-aged, unmarried, orphaned niece, of a retired socialite.

"*Almost* like a daughter" indeed, but hardly a substitute for Jasper, her only son, father unknown. Bernice felt sure that Jasper was delaying adult maturity, in order to play chaperone to his mother, until she attended her last party, the one in the funeral parlour. Then he would inherit 'Freedom Cottage', Mavis's idyllic country home, with aplomb.

As she poured another drink, Bernice smarted at the thought of 'Freedom Cottage' being left in the profligate hands of Jasper. What ridiculous schemes would he carry out? If he were out of the way, Bernice would be in line to inherit it herself, as the only other living relative.

"*Almost* a daughter, indeed!" yowled Bernice aloud. She often spoke out loud to herself, as who could begrudge her the voicing of her darker thoughts? There was no-one to hear because she lived alone in a converted barn, which she used as her pottery studio. (Pottery gave her something to do with her hands when she wasn't drinking). Oh the things she could do, if she inherited Freedom Cottage! She could develop a pottery and tea-room franchise, (with the baking outsourced), tables lain with her own handiwork. She would serve beer in the flower gardens in the summer. "Oh dear, I'm talking to myself again", she mused, seeing she had finished all the whiskey. "I must be getting lonely."

In times of emotional and other crises, Bernice would telephone her lover, Franklin Fanshawe, Barrister at Law. As Mavis's legal counsel, he doubled up nicely as a lover for Bernice, trading 'insider' secrets, in exchange for Bernice's pottery 'love-knots.' She would really put him through his paces today, after Mavis's latest caper! "Franklin, get ready, I'll be right over. We need to discuss Mavis's affairs", Bernice spluttered down the line, her speech slightly slurred. She didn't wait for a reply. Franklin was always ready to receive her in his 'high-end' apartment, where he took respite from his travails at the Bar.

Bernice attempted to make herself presentable for the meeting. She hadn't inherited the same genes as Mavis, when it came to delicate beauty. Instead, she "made the most of herself", as Mavis had often cajoled.

"That'll do the trick", she pronounced to her reflection in the mirror, as she slashed a line of pink lipstick across her lips. She tried not to notice the sets of bags under her eyes, accompanying her waxen, lined complexion. She felt sure her brown blow-wave compensated for her face, as she ran her fingers through it. Mavis had pointed out that Bernice had acquired "the face she deserved", thanks to her peccadilloes. Bernice had locked herself away for days afterwards, wailing aloud, and imbibing whiskey chasers. The news of Mavis's hospitalisation was just enough to jolt her back to reality again.

Although she shouldn't be driving, being currently "under the influence", she jumped into her car, nudging the empty bottles underfoot. The car rattled as she drove; the glass orchestra of the clinking bottles, adding an extra tension to her thoughts.

From his apartment window, Franklin heard the loud screeching of brakes, the steering being strangled into submission, which announced Bernice's arrival. He could tell it was Bernice without so much as a glimpse, and surmised what kind of mood she was in. He had the coffee machine percolating, when she thundered through his door, with the ominous announcement 'She's done it again!" Slumping onto the leather couch, placing her feet upon the glass table, she dismounted his barristers wig off its stand.

"What *has* she done again?" Franklin enquired innocently, as he placed a strong coffee on front of her. He knew full well that Bernice was in a belligerent mood, and that she had Mavis in her sights.

"She's still *alive*", Bernice spat. "Will I ever be free of her?" She started to sob great rivulets of tears as she attempted to gulp her coffee. "If only there was a way that Freedom Cottage would be mine. Jasper can't be trusted with such a responsibility, being the rake he is. Goodness, he'll drag the place to rack and ruin."

Another long sob, and then glowering at Franklin, she said stealthily; "If you can help me inherit it, there will be compensation for you. It must be worth a couple of million, being thatched Tudor-style, with its rare flower gardens." She banged down her coffee cup, leaving an imprint of lipstick on the rim.

Franklin considered his options, brushing the dandruff from the collar of his pin-striped jacket. Perhaps it was time to put an end to his playboy lifestyle, and be taken more seriously at the Bar. (Lord knows, he had spent enough time at the other type of bar!)

Something stirred his conscience.

"Bernice", he said, clearing his throat, "Mavis came to see me earlier, before she was detained by the hospital, as it were. She would like to will Freedom Cottage to Jasper, to be run as a Cat's Home. And the final nail in the coffin..." he paused for effect, basking in his own cleverness, "...is that there is a sealed letter left for *you*, to be opened after her passing."

He turned his face away from her to conceal his grin.

Bernice was astounded. In a brief moment, she saw her life flash on front of her. Her drinking, and reckless love affairs had left little time to get her 'house in order'. By now in her mid-forties, she was eager to acquire more assets, allowing herself a comfortable retirement. If Franklin did not want to be part of the plan, then that was *his* mischance.

"Freedom Cottage will be turned into a cat's home over my *dead* body! After all, I'm *almost* a daughter. She said so herself. I deserve my share!" she cried. Franklin glibly pointed out that Mavis was still of sound mind, and she was perfectly free to leave the cottage to Jasper. There was no reason not to turn it into a Cats Home. "In fact, that's wonderfully philanthropic of her", he teased.

"She *hates* cats!" Bernice banged down her coffee cup once more. With dismay she noticed a crack appearing along its side, appalled that it was one of her own pottery samples. She changed the subject to avert Franklin's attention from her shoddy wares.

"What was that letter you mentioned?" she barked. Franklin paused for effect for the second time (as if he were in the court room). "All will be revealed, in due course", he said smugly.

"Forget our appointment; I have other business to attend to!" Bernice issued her parting shot before racing out. She kick-started her car into action, and sped off towards Freedom Cottage, empty bottles jangling underfoot once more. Her priorities were firmly intact.

With any luck, Jasper would still be at Mavis's hospital bedside. What on earth was that letter that Franklin was talking about? And hadn't Mavis always teased that Jasper would get 'the keys to the door', on his fortieth birthday?

Bernice increased her pedal power, when it dawned on her that Jasper's fortuitous birthday was the following week; making an emergency stop at a garage, she purchased a bottle of whiskey and a bunch of flowers, in order to ply his weaknesses. "Beware of Greeks bearing Gifts", she said out loud as she swerved dangerously around the bend towards Freedom Cottage.

She inhaled the luxuriant scent of the lush gardens leading to Mavis's front door. Using the whiskey bottle as a lance, she hacked her way through the dense hedges of roses, lavender and foxglove, wending their way up the garden path. Reaching the front door, she let herself in with the spare key kept under the Grecian-style pottery urn outside (another sample of her handiwork).

Surveying the inside of the cottage, its low-beamed ceilings, antique furniture, and a high fireplace, Berenice wanted it all for herself. She would have Mavis declared insane, and Jasper as mentally incompetent, if need be.

Shaking loose the sheaves of pages in each book on the tall bookshelves, she sought to find and destroy the letter that Franklin had told her about, leaving no evidence of Mavis' plans for a Cat's Home. Really, it beggared belief!

Frantic and dusty, she tentatively poked her large hands into the nooks and crannies at the fireplace, finally uncovering a sealed envelope displaying Bernice's date of birth, some forty-five years previously, written on the front. At the antique kitchen table, she unsealed the bottle of whiskey she had brought, before ripping open the envelope. She recognised the lavender ink that Mavis always used.

"Dear Bernice, By the time you read this, I will have passed to more tranquil pastures. I have a confession to make. I have loved you like a daughter, second only to Jasper. ("Ha!" snorted Bernice). You were adopted by my sister because your mother could not keep you. She was a beautiful model in London, the toast of the town. Can you imagine the scandal if it were announced that she was pregnant out of wedlock?

That model was me. I returned to Ireland, and arranged your adoption. I only ask that you are kind to me, after the fact. Jasper will legally inherit Freedom Cottage to be used as a Cat's Home, undersigned by Franklin. I am leaving you my favourite piece of jewellery to remember me by. Please do not put my true age on my gravestone. Mavis"

....

Her head reeling with shock and whiskey, Bernice drove wildly around the bend. Her car hit a cat, and hurtled downwards into a ditch. Bernice lay slumped against the wheel, at precisely the moment Mavis's heart gave out in her hospital bed.

Bernice felt a hand brush her cheek, and saw Mavis at her side. Then through the darkness, she heard the police sirens. "Daughter", whispered Mavis, leaving a lingering scent of lavender, before vanishing.

Dancing Queen

The showgirl is missing! echoed in hushed tones, throughout the backstage area at the Fog and Horn Theatre.

Bobby and Vinnie, the Brothers Brimm, were faced with an unforeseen dilemma. Bunny Bordella, the leading lady, and burlesque artiste supreme, was missing from their line-up. The ransom note attached to the lightbulb-festooned mirror in her dressing room, was addressed to the "Leaders of the Pack."

Bobby, the elder brother and Principal Pianist, read the note aloud, turning his back on Vinnie. They had not spoken directly to each other in years, neither for love nor for money.

Bunny has been taken captive. She will not be returned to the cast, unless the princely sum of €1,000 plus expenses, and a souvenir from among her risqué costumes, is deposited in a skip outside the theatre's rear-door. In the event of non-payment, there will be untoward repercussions.

Alone together in Bunny's dressing room; surrounded by items of her stage apparel, and vials of scents, powders and paints, each brother suspected the other of this farcical ploy.

Bunny's plight forced their hand. Both already knew that the show was on its last legs, and Bunny's burlesque solo was its last main attraction. If they had wanted a Murder Mystery night instead, they would have hired someone else!

Should we pay or should we keep our change? asked Vinnie. Bunny and he had been 'involved' for the past few weeks. She had taken pity on him when she found him sleeping off a hangover, in the *very* skip, mentioned in the ransom note. Vinnie was the Comedian of the Company, who could make her laugh *and* cry, during after-show whiskey sessions, where both mirth and melancholy flowed easily. However, Bobby was more flamboyant than his brother; it was atop his ivory piano that Bunny danced every night onstage. The brothers were unaware there was an extra 'cog' in the wheel, in the form of Russ Lovell, the Violinist. He had been hired to add a romantic dimension to the show. And so he did! His affair with Bunny began between the First and Second Acts, on the opening night.

First things first! Bobby picked up the phone, to inform the Stage Manager, *The show will go ahead <u>without</u> the Leading Lady, and Bunny's role will be filled by none other than myself. I shall have to 'rein it in' and* *improvise during the striptease section. The theatre is dark, and the audience will be too drunk to notice...*

But what of the ransom money? Business taken care of, the brothers broke years of resentful silence, each hailing a torrent of insults at the other.

Perhaps you should cough up all the money. You've being trying to muscle in for some time on my love interest, accused Vinnie

I've done nothing of the sort retorted Bobby. *There were damages incurred when you tossed Bunny a little too loftily on top of my piano for the burlesque scene. We'll call it quits if you cover the ransom money.*

No Way! shouted Vinnie. *What about my unpaid Royalties? Where have you been laundering all the takings?*

This show is costly, hissed Bobby, *someone has to be responsible for our welfare. And it's certainly not you. Falling down drunk on stage every night! However, the Show must go on. We'll come to a gentleman's agreement later.*

The air was heavy with suspense as the brothers burst forth from the dressing room, each to take his position in the wings. The show *must* go on.

Prelude

The previous day, Bunny and Bobby were alone in Bobby's cramped dressing room. She was dressed in a worn-out ensemble of sequins, feather and lace, as she approached Bobby while he tinkled softly on his miniature piano. Bunny had taken to arriving at work in her costumes, in order to allot herself more 'rehearsal' time; often coming to the theatre breathless and unkempt.

Bobby, I need an advance on my wages, she said in slightly shrill voice. Bobby looked up absentmindedly, seeming to look right through her, his eyes reflecting the sparkle of her sequins. *Bobby, I need money. Fast!* said Bunny, getting up close and personal. Bobby continued playing 'Dancing Queen', their showpiece together, where she danced seductively to his tune. At this moment, however, there was a thorny issue raising its ugly head.

She climbed into position on his piano lid, placing a kitten-heel shoe across the keyboard as he played.

There's no 'dough' until the show finishes, Bunny. We're all in the same boat, I'm afraid, Sweetie. With an abrupt snapping shut of the piano lid, the subject also seemed to be closed. He looked up at her, in an attempt at sincerity, and then he noticed her.

dishevelled appearance. Her mascara was running; her costume ripped.

What happened to your costume Bunny? You're getting through your glad rags like no one's business! We can't afford to keep you in these rig-outs, my dear. Bobby was not impressed. *I'm afraid some of your fee shall be deducted for wear and tear.*

Bunny felt her pulse quicken. *I've got nothing else to wear. No mon, no fun*! she snapped. It was as if Bobby had slapped her across her bare cheek. She stamped her heel as she continued in an injured tone, *As a matter of pressing concern, Bobby, I am going to withdraw from the show. Money's so tight (and so are you,* she muttered under her breath*), that I'm going to have to take on a better job where the cash is upfront.* In a firm voice, she added, *I'm a working girl, you know, and a girl's got to live a little.*

Sensing her disquiet, Bobby attempted to make light of the situation. He had some affection for Bunny, and did not want the show to run out of steam without Bunny's show-stoppers. After all, they were only ever as good as their last review.

I'll try and sort something out, but these things take <u>time</u>. The Piper doesn't get paid until we're done. Another three weeks 'til closing. Surely you can hold out that long, he stroked the inside of Bunny's wrist lightly.

Bunny's costume tore slightly again, as her temper rose. She knew she was a lucky girl to work with the Brimm Brothers, and the auditions had been rigorous, each of the brothers really putting her through her paces. She had proved herself a good all-rounder, and she felt she must be paid her dues. *Bobby, I never intended to be a starving artist. I got into this game in the first place, because I've got enough chutzpah to know that I've a good set of pipes, and the ability to work my best assets.*

Bobby hated it when she attempted to be slightly cleverer than was necessary. She was still *'arriviste'* in his estimation, and it was he who had brought out the best she had to give. Without his guidance, and his accompanying piano showpieces, she would be ordinary; yet another glamour girl seeking to see her name in lights, and with scant ability for the hard graft, and personal sacrifice it took to get to the top of the heap.

He didn't want to cut her loose just yet, however. He had an unspoken understanding of a showgirl's concerns, as Bunny discovered during their many heart-to-heart discussions about costumes, makeup, dance routines, and above all, the fecklessness of her many suitors.

Darling, I'd take you out tonight to discuss your money trouble, but I haven't got a stitch to wear and neither have you, he said, indicating the growing rip in the seams of her costume. *The fact is; we're all trying to break even. No-one around here gets paid 'til closing night. The whole troupe is dressed in hand me downs from the Retired Performers Home, except for you, in your custom-made finery."*

His eye caught the flailing swish of her tail feather. *Was Vinnie rough with you again? He's bringing up the charge sheet, and down the wages; the amount of expenses he racks up, thanks to his inebriated antics. Brother Dearest is a liability.*

Bunny perceived that perhaps Bobby had troubles of his own, so she reluctantly let the matter drop for now. *Alright, Bobby, I'll just slip into something more comfortable,* she said, getting behind the ornate changing screen, which just about concealed her from view. She quickly flung her sequined, feathered, and lace leotard over the top, while continuing her conversation. *Don't worry about the money. It'll sort itself out.* This seemed like an opportune moment for Bobby to change his tune, whilst Bunny momentarily paused in her adjustments. She was more than ready to negotiate her terms, should he be willing.

Bobby flitted to the screen door, gallantly averting his eyes, and fetched the costume carefully. He had reassumed his piano seat, when Bunny emerged a few moments later in her evening wear of leather, with matching biker's cap. Blowing a kiss in his direction, she bid him good evening. *Ta ra, Bobby, I'm off now, see you tomorrow night,* she said nonchalantly. Best to keep him sweet, she thought. She did know on what side her bread was buttered, after all.

For some time after she left, Bobby sat caressing her costume. In the half-light he lifted it against his silhouette, imbibing the scent of her cheap perfume. *Nothing a little lycra wouldn't fix,* he whispered to himself. He decided he needed to get out too, and exited the dressing room. He knew a backstreet costumier, who owed him a favour, and could alter the costume.

Lycra's the way to go from now on. We must stretch these costumes to their last, he thought to himself, as he cradled Bunny's costume over his arm, the broken tail feather dangling limply from the peacock's plume. *We must cut our cloth according to its measure.*

It had been an audacious move on Bobby's behalf, but somehow, he had delivered a swansong that Bunny would have been proud of. He was borne offstage on the shoulders of Vinnie, and Russ Lovell, to rapturous applause. Standing in the wings, he felt like an angel in gossamer.

To Hell with Bunny, we'll go it alone, he declared to his stage manager. No longer would he be the impresario bolstering other people's ambitions. As if the spirit of Bunny had inhabited him when he donned her costume, now her ghost had left the building and the limelight shone elsewhere.

Vinnie exited the stage, and collapsed in a heap in the corner. The stage manager duly rushed to get him something stiff from the bar.

All's well that ends well, said Bobby as he watched the violinist deliver the closing torch song.

Another one bites the dust! was all Vinnie could muster. There seemed to be a complicit agreement that they sacrifice Bunny.

Shall we shake on this? asked Bobby.

Agreed!, replied Vinnie, extending a hand to shake Bobby's, and the other to accept his drink.

We don't need any unclaimed baggage, was Bobby's summation of the entire farce. Already they were a box office hit, and would be retained by the Fog and Horn indefinitely.

Bunny's whereabouts were never revealed, but the rumour mill revealed that she had been down on her luck, and had numerous creditors.

Opening his vintage Louis Vuitton suitcase backstage one night, Bobby felt a pang of regret at Bunny's loss. Inside the suitcase were all the fine costumes that Bunny had worn her way through. Bobby had restored them in bespoke lace and gold to his own silhouette.

In the cheap tabloid he had hidden among the costumes, the headline declared "Body on Beach Murder enquiry! Death in Leather and Feathers"

What happened to you, my lovely? whispered Bobby.

He snapped shut the suitcase as a lone peacock feather flitted out towards him.

Bunny's Farewell

Jennifer Kissane

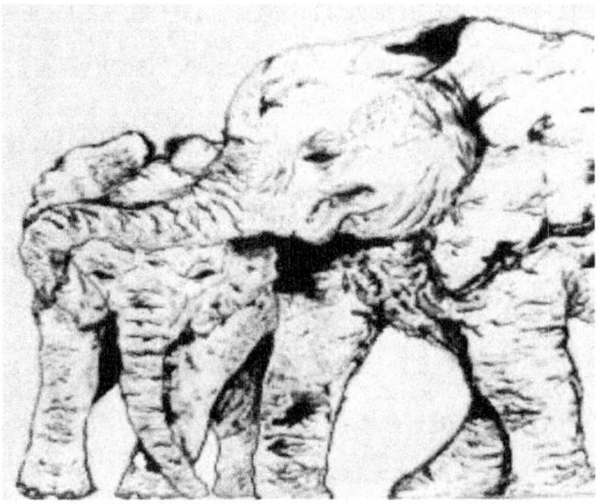

The soul becomes dyed with the colour of its thoughts

- Marcus Aurelius.

Living in rural Ireland, Jennifer Kissane has previously resided in the UK, working in the TV industry. Three of her short stories have been published by *Yours* magazine (Bauer Media UK).

In 2022, she has joined the *AsIam* (Ireland's Autism Charity) Creative Writing Group, which reignited a passion for writing. Jennifer's work tends to be grounded in the exploration of personal relationships and 'what ifs'. She finds it both exhilarating and cathartic to explore the myriad of possibilities of the human psyche. Writing mostly prose, since 2021 Jennifer has dabbled in poetry. Art, nature and dogs provide a backdrop to much of her work.

You are on my mind

a flickering shadow

on the thoughts of the day

afternoons spent together

hand in hand

apple trees   burnt toast

the sun on the land

your broad back   my constant view

afternoons of muddy knees

sticky grilled cheese

jokes being played

{at my expense}

simple times

stretched out for years

our past is in my head

shimmering in this light

the feel of your tweed jacket

tickling my freckled cheek

we never really talked about then

too caught up in the here and now

i wish we had

it wouldn't have taken long

to laugh   recall

whitewashing walls

a donkey foal

fresh cut grass

little red wellies

forever getting stuck in holes

Rebirth

morning rises with a barley sun

peeking through muslin

in impish delight

dancing a wedding polka

on canvas white walls

daring   cajoling

a wearied body to rise

bask in the warmth

of nature's embrace

allow muddy rumination

to melt into the morning dew

to sip beneath blackened soil

leaving pure naked truth

without blemish or burden

refreshed

reborn

Belonging

There are days when the world is too loud, too bright, or too coarse.

Impossible to make people understand what it feels to be squeezed, stung, and shouted at by everything around me.

Always my existence, that naively it has taken me years to realise that not everyone experiences the world with such intensity.

Fabric can pierce to the extent I expect to see lacerations when I remove the offending garment.

The levels of voices around me reverberate around my skull like dozens of incorrectly tuned radios.

Lights – blinding.

Bodies in the supermarket too close. I retreat to the empty aisles, longing for social distancing to be mandatory again.

When this tidal wave overwhelms me, escape is vital. Either to velvet of darkness or to nature.

Usually, I am good at masking it. In fact, I can be an expert. When it escapes, it is like trying to control the flow of the Amazon. The shame afterwards comes with equal force, a grown woman who acts as overwrought as a toddler.

Sitting on the garden bench, there is a sense of peace. A bug scurries across the grey cement, disappearing down a crack in the joining. The dog nuzzles my hand for a pat, the coldness of her nose, bringing me back from the depths. Her triangular ears perked. Eyes gleaming like melted chocolate. She pushes her head under my palm.

Go on, she appeals, *give me a scratch.*

I do.

Ebony fur soft and glossy, having just been brushed. The rhythm and repetition regulating my breathing.

Yippee, she seems to say when she sees the green brush in my hand. Athletic bounces to the bench to begin her beauty regiment.

Little does she know I do it as much for me as for her. This little dog is cheaper than my therapist but has provided me with essential coping skills. The unity of the relationship creates a place where I fit, no self-adjustment required. I can be as I am. She loves me regardless. Her wagging tail brings me joy.

Conversation is easy. There is no talking too much or too little; too loud or too soft. An easy companionship, where neither of us must overthink our behaviour. No pretence or secret language to strive to understand. When I stop petting her, she paws my knee. An apt example of her clear precise communication! She is quite the comedian this collie. The ease of a small laugh fills my bones with warmth. There is no time for indulgence, she is insistent. A second pawing tells me to tickle her ears. She has become my anchor in the ebbs and flows of an unsteady world. An easy nature, soothing me in these moments when the world is too heavy.

Behind my sunglasses, the mountains are splashed with greens, browns, and purples. I have often felt some deity dropped their palette, resulting in the splendour of the MacGillycuddy Reeks. Jagged outlines create a firm boundary for the colours swirling within. They are a speckled mix of sheep and rocks. The dog at my feet used to herd sheep on that range, her paws pounding the uneven ground; ears twitching in the direction of my father's bellowed instructions. Those days are gone. My father has passed; his companion has become my companion. So many memories entwined in this bundle of fur. She used to hold sentry at his feet in his later years, alert, waiting for him to summon her to the flock. There is suspicion in our clan that despite her obedience, she always held aspirations of being something more pampered, liked a shih tzu, a pomeranian or one of the late Queen's corgis.

The evidence for this identity crisis?

She embraced wearing a Christmas jumper much too readily and would sit eagerly for her reindeer gansey to be put on. She would strut her stuff with the confidence of a model on the Paris runway wearing Haute Couture until the second of January.

We sit in stillness; her eyes are closed, soaking in the afternoon sun. The weight of her body rests against my shin. I breathe deeply, urging the battle in me to find peace on the fresh air. Looking toward the garden and the mountains, I do that exercise of finding colours in the environment, which I've been told helps in these moments.

Find something yellow. The blossoms of the fir bushes in the fields.

Find something blue. The sky. It is bright and clear.

Find something black. The flowerpot.

I pause. There are two butterflies dancing in the air. Their strange two-step looks cartoonish. Underneath their fluttering wings, the grass needs mowing. Small wildflowers have sprung up. I smile at a memory of being very young and my brother showing me that "the daisies go to sleep at night." I imagined them yawning around dinnertime. Fascinated by these slumbering blooms, I would try to catch them in the act of nodding off.

Closing my eyes and absorbing the soundscape. The flow of the nearby river whispers on the air. The robin's merry tune is nearby. A car passes breaking the solitude and the meditation. The dog raises her head, decides it isn't an emergency and puts it back onto her outstretched paws.

Time to get up, I say to myself and her.

Neither of us move. I still can feel the wet of the tears on my face; embarrassment fills me. My heart begins to race again.

BOOM! BOOM! BOOM!

I can do this, I say, *this is nothing, just a difficult day.*

A day when everything is too loud.

A day when I can't explain the turmoil within.

What causes this distress is also what allows me to experience the world differently. Endows me with a unique brand of creativity, serving me well professionally. Thinking outside the box because not every box is the same.

My fluffy friend stretches reluctantly, her rump rising and then falling as she does a perfect Yoga pose. Opening her jaws wide to yawn.

I've not regained my equilibrium yet but feeling the caress of the wind, in a wide-open space and embracing life has helped. The volume on those radios in my brain has been lowered, if not muted.

I can function again.

I pat the dog. We go toward the door.

I'll work through my list for the day. Everything will find its place.

Nature shows us every element has its individual brushstroke making life a masterpiece.

Luke McCormac Parker

What may be, with patience

Originally from Dublin, Ireland, Luke McCormac Parker spends most of his time still there. He is a member of the *Write So!* Creative Writing Group through *AsIAm.* Writing short stories from childhood, primarily a fiction writer inspired by fantasy, sci-fi and horror, he has also made forays into poetry. These pieces in this anthology will be his first published creative works. He hopes to keep writing and having his work published.

Cold Road

~ Stimulus: write a piece from the song title
Cold Road by Chinx ~

I've waited over an hour here
stood shifting foot to foot for vain reprieve
sleet sliding under clothing, heat leaching
bleaching skin shiver-white
a golden chariot turns the corner
heat and shelter of the bus
promises home after this ever-longer day
but not for me   wrong number
the others crowd aboard
I contemplate my life choices as I huddle by the exhaust
Warming myself in the noxious fumes
to brace against the all-too fresh air
as I wait still more

Broken Frame

On a table deep within sits a picture frame
Sometimes it is facing away, othertimes lain flat
When it is coldest, damp to bone
The source can be found on the table
Placidly glaring back

No picture lies within the frame
Broken glass shards like frost on wood
Off-white backing staring out
Attend as would a lighthouse lantern
All traced with stains of old blood

My fingers ache with chill and old cuts
Memory of scars, scars of memory
From each time I try to puzzle out the frame
What portrait does it portend
Who gouged it out, when and why

I know only that within lay a picture of myself
Faded photograph of who I was
Promiseful painting of who I ought
I can no longer recall either being there
Or what they would look like if so

In dreary dreams I imagine
Furtively approaching the empty frame
Smashing the intact glass
Struggling to fit something behind
Leaving with crumpled attempt in bloody hand

In bleakest thoughts it occurs to me
That the pane is shattered sharp
That the frame is shallow, hollow
That no person is to be found
There sits my perfect self-portrait

The Envelope

~ written in seven minutes
in response to a class stimulus ~

The envelope in the post-box had no address, no stamp.

Just a key and a train ticket.

The key was marked 'HX-286', which Alisa recognised as belonging to one of the maintenance cabinets in the basement. As for the ticket, it made no sense to her, despite being an inveterate resident of the station.

Curiosity being better than boredom, she explored the night-stilled halls looking for the cabinet.

Finding it in one of the underground tunnels, the angular key clicked as it turned. The cabinet doors groaned open to reveal not a series of electronics, but a tunnel.

Anxiousness being better than despair, Alisa followed the dark hallway.

To her utter confusion she found herself in a tall chamber, opening into the night sky.

A wrought iron staircase led to the doors of a train set vertically on one wall. Markings on one open door matched her ticket.

As she approached, a set of tracks began to extend upwards toward the starry sky.

The 'tard and Feathered

To some we are misbegotten homunculi,
Pitiable poppets, puzzles to jigsaw,
At least a piece less than human,
Blemishes to be politely concealed

They speak in our name, pilfering non-verbal of voices,
Claiming to search for autism's resolution,
We know they merely seek an excuse,
A demure return to Asperger's solution

To some we are malignant parasites,
Tumours upon Their economy,
Devouring without contributing,
Drooling on the Self-Made mythos

They insist that the burden is in the supports,
Our vulgar needs denying their refined aspirations,
And for the greater good must Atlas shrug,
Correcting the deficits of death and taxes

To some we are enabled infants,
Acting out for wanton wants,
Symptoms of a Western plague,
Dedicated vocations of inconvenience

They turnabout and spoil the rod,
Hammer out proud nails of the Ark,
Self-appointed painful pedagogues,
Saviours of civilization

We cannot be what they want,
For they want us not to be,
The only compromise they'll settle for,
Us adorning their Day of the Rope

It does not start with hate but pity,
Humanity dislodged in increments,
Granting the momentum to extremity,
Shifting society's weight towards the worst

Our masks are mirrors, protective prosthetics,
They wear theirs to hide the hideous,
In denial of their ideals' inhumanity,
Willing the unconscionable to the unconscious

Who are they to bar the gate to Society,
Or stamp the visas to Validity,
Or with flick of pen and click of mouse,
To turn disabled to debilitated

By what standard do they rally,
Some fallacy of naturality,
Normativity's manifest destiny,
Or just false bravado of the status quo

Those fervent prisoners of preconception,
So comfortable in their confines they resent
Implications that there's anything beyond,
That their walls aren't the world

We shouldn't have to Other ourselves,
Relegating inner identities to Outsiders,
We need not dance their masquerade,
Though our smiles ache and our feet bleed

We need not be forlorn on our paths,
Wandering blaring streets or secluded trails,
Lost at every crossroad, alone,
But for our creeping pursuer

We can instead walk with each other,
Be it side-by-side or just in spirit,
Stride strong in heart and number our roads to Home,
Intersected with Rose, Yellow Brick or Damascene

We must be us if we are
To make and take our places,
To be a part of it not apart from it,
Whether they want us or not, we are

We must be us
For we can truly be none other,
Fated like all to live within ourselves,
So we might as well act like it

Cian Morey

You must go on, I can't go on, I'll go on.

Originally from Cork, Ireland, Cian Morey (he/him) is a writer of short stories, very short plays, and even shorter poems. His prose fiction has been published in *The Mays*, *The Leaves*, *The Irish Times*, *The RTÉ Guide* and *The Listowel Writers' Week Anthology*.

His work has won the Listowel Writers' Week Youth Writing Competition and the Puffin/RTÉ Guide Young People's Writing Competition, and has been shortlisted or longlisted for contests including the Colm Tóibín Short Story Award, the H.G. Wells Short Story Competition, the Scribes Prize and the Oxford Flash Fiction Prize.

He has read at literary events or has had plays performed in Cork, Kerry and Cambridge. He writes chiefly for his own entertainment and, if he's lucky, for the entertainment of others. Inspirations for his writing range from cinema to visual art, from science fiction of the far-flung future to music from before he was born.

When he is not writing fiction he is usually making the bad decision to write stand-up comedy, or the even worse decision to perform it.

A Heartfelt Goodbye

I, being of sound mind and body, hereby wilfully and voluntarily request that my property, estates, and personal effects, shall all pass to absolutely no one.

To my ex-wife Deborah, in loving memory of the agonising years we endured in each other's company, and in heartfelt recognition of all of the kindness she did not show me during our slow and acrimonious divorce, I hereby leave nothing.

To my estranged brother Ebenezer, who has always been there to support anyone but me during the countless difficult periods of my life, I hereby leave my entire collection of absolutely nothing.

To my sister Lilith, who made many important memories with me throughout my life - none of them good - I hereby leave nothing whatsoever.

Finally, to my son: I am sorry that we have not seen eye to eye, ever since that day you blinded me, just as I am sorry that you are almost certainly responsible for my inevitable murder. I hereby leave you the remaining sum total of nothing at all, to dispense with as you please.

And, for myself, I leave this mortal coil with all possible haste, and about time too.

Rotten Fruit

The Man was in my dream again.

A marketplace this time, thick with tourists and bright with unnameable fruit, in some sunny dreamland that had splashed the lush tree-lined boulevards of central Paris into the dry canvas of cobbled squares and squat old churches of the Mediterranean. It could have been charming.

But the Man would be there.

I didn't know where, or when, and certainly not how, but I knew He would be there. It didn't matter the setting — in the past or the future, at home or across the globe, lost among strangers or laughing among friends, wherever my dream dropped me, there He would be, somewhere, however distant or brief, but there He would be.

The sun got into my eyes in every direction I faced. I glanced over the jabbering crowd, glimpsing so many more faces than I could possibly scrutinise, judging whom I could elbow and shove out of my path if I needed to run. Hawkers bellowed about their wares in all the wrong languages, promising 'beaux poissons', 'Schwarzbrot', 'pomodoro'. I shuffled to a nearby stall. Not looking the seller in the face, I took an innocent orange from a tray, and there He was, His oily left eye looking up at me like a rotten fruit.

Family Man

'Cocktail, sir?' asks the most melodious voice that Alberto has ever heard.

He shifts on his deckchair to see a statuesque waitress standing over him with a tray of cavernous martini glasses. The rim of every glass twinkles with crystalled sunlight like a show of tiny fireworks.

'What?' Alberto says.

'Cocktail, sir,' the waitress repeats, and takes one off the tray, as if to say, 'They're real, honestly - look.'

Alberto looks. A stout olive bobs on the surface like a millionaire drowned in his own swimming pool.

Alberto waves the waitress away with a flick of one hand, then starts to apologise, then gives up, and lies with his foot tapping on the floor and his fingers picking a hole in the deckchair canvas. He glances down the row of seats and notes the company he is somehow in. One woman is talking uninhibitedly of how her maid never folds her cashmere jumpers properly in the walk-in wardrobe. A man with a pocket square is trying to ascertain from the waitress whether there are any oysters onboard. Everyone has taken a martini.

Alberto repositions himself on the deckchair, feels his lower back strain over the sagging canvas, tries to organise his limbs into a more comfortable posture. He can't fit himself comfortably into his new identity either. There is a passport in his pocket with a picture of his face above another man's signature. The pages, carefully stamped with too little ink or too many smudges for the tell-tale details to be legible, pretend that he is a wealthy hotel owner, well-travelled in France, Austria and England - or possibly Finland - or is it Poland?

'Can I practice the signature?' Alberto had asked, when the Family had tucked the passport into his breast pocket.

'Relax, *fratello*,' the Consigliere had told him. 'You have the rest of your life to practice the signature.'

Beyond the boat's softly rocking bow, the water glows a perfect turquoise and stretches to a cloudless horizon. Alberto doesn't know what he expected. Did he think thunder and lightning would come to signal that he was making the wrong choice? Did he think his irresolvable doubts would bring dark sies and unnavigable seas? The world as he sees it now is unmoved by his writhing conscience. The weather does not care. The journey seems easy, even appealing. There is nothing in the indifferent face of heaven or earth to make his mind up for him.

He can see on the coast a black limousine and a man in a suit too dark for this sun standing and waving to him like a mother dropping a child off to school. The Family has never looked more familial.

'I wanted to kill you, *amico,*' the Consigliere had told him, and then howled in laughter, a second too late. 'No, no, just joking. It's important to joke, ha? Everything is okay. They are giving you another chance. *Sì*. Me, I would have killed you - aha! I got you again - but they said, Let him make a new life. *Sì*. Remember that, *fratello* - they said that. And what is a family for, if not to forgive?'

An involuntary trembling; the boat starts to move. The limousine back on land starts to shrink. Alberto thinks of old wounds fading. The man with the pocket square is now miming an oyster as he struggles to explain himself to the waitress. Alberto breathes in and out, feels the punch of the gun stuffed into his jacket lining. If he stays onboard, there's a villa paid for him in Greece with a sea view and a promise of new beginnings. If he goes back, it's a shootout. He calls for a cocktail after all. Steady the nerves.

Dave Murphy

From, and returned to Wicklow, Ireland via adventures in other lands, Dave has worked in music, sound and words all his life. A lover of poetry and short stories, he also reads a lot of academic works and technical manuals. He has performed in Ireland, Europe and USA. This is his first foray into the world of flash fiction. He finds delight in the use of everyday language in the world at large; a word used well being a thing of joy.

Bus

Every day he hauled himself into the uncomfortable seat and he drove and drove. All the back roads, all the byroads, all the bloody roads of this dismal town.

For years now the same circuit, same route, picking them up, setting them down until he reaches the turn at the end of her road.

He never knows if she will travel today, into town, out of town, further into his heart or out of his life.

For years now this gentle-glanced hope, spotted he thinks, reciprocated her wishes.

Next week he retires.

Speak or hold his peace?

What peace there is with this longing, yearning heart

Boat

I am not Robinson Crusoe.

I'm lost here for sure. How many days now? Is it days or am I lost to some dream time?
It sank, I know it sank. How else can I be here?
Cold now, grey below, above, in every direction.

There is land, but craggy rocks and sheer cliffs and no place for ashore.
I'm floating north I think, I can feel it.
I hear the ice-cracks reflecting off the grey arc of this chilling sky.
I will sleep a bit, it might be late.

There is a warm comfort in my freezing bones, alone.

She will come for me, save me. Love me back to life.

I hear her on the breeze. I taste her salty kiss on my lips.

I will go to her, she will save me.
This selkie, this siren, this sea

Hunt

An impressive rubble pile indeed, he thought, but whose idea was it to lean the grain store right up against the gable wall of the main house?

The crunch underfoot of kernels dragged across flagstone floors lent a rustic touch. The scent of roasting oats from that which rested on the other side of the wall from the fireplace warmed the air.

This nod to the medieval was a little crass.

All this was well and good. But unbothered, Smittens confidently, proudly honed his claws on the strop of his tongue.

He could smell the mouse blood to come, taste their guts.

His eyes glinted.

Narrowed.

Let the carnage begin.

Ann Ryan

Ann is new to creative writing and part of the group Write So!, a zoom creative writing group with AsIAm. Inspired by nature, art and music, she uses imagery to best describe how she's feeling - like crawling & curling up into her protective shell, like a snail, when needing to refuel or recharge if the world is too much, until ready to poke her head out again and venture out. This process is also useful for her in creative writing, and when trying to silence her inner critic. Through writing, as an outlet for her emotions, she also wants to get to know herself better. To listen and nourish the voice within.

Moments

dawning morning sun
shimmering light
birds in flight alight
tree branches
rooftops
chirping cooing
auditory delight

clothesline full flapping
curling fingers round
hot cup of tea
cookie crumbling
after being dipped
blown bubbles bursting
kerb kids laughing

walking through woods
scarf wrapped neck
hat covered head
leaves crunch underfoot
ferns unfurling fronds
trees teeming skywards
sun dappled colours
scattered fluffy clouds

evening comes brightly
fiery sunset blazing
trailing the sky
nature's colours abound
surround
both palette & canvas
wondrous paintings
displayed

sitting snug
fire crackling
rain pitter patters
outside
wind howling
window rattling
curled up with a book

RAGE

Intense raw emotion

fuelled up inside

frustration building bubbling

anger seething boiling blistering

ready to burst forth unleashing

body tense, worked up

coiled tight like a

spring to be sprung

laying down layers

volcano ready to erupt

wanting to scream, shout

vent and let it out

release all the tension

quell the fire within

calm my senses

make it all disappear

rewind & avoid

now curled in a ball

in the dark   upset

not understanding what happened

my reaction   emotions

ashamed of the spill & spew forth

how to move on

regain some sense of self

soothe and settle

reassure - it's alright

little girl within

Oh my dear child

quiet shy unsure

what would I say to you now?

when school days were hard back then

what would have helped?

to pass on the wisdom experience

I've gained over these years

to silence those internal fears

Have confidence & self esteem

it's ok to be you

don't mind what others say

pay no heed don't let it in!

hold your head high

follow your own path

stay true to yourself

keep doing you

have belief in yourself

You're doing the best you can
do not turn on yourself
or hate   love yourself instead
be your own best friend

I want to bring you forward
take you by the hand,
as we laugh   skip & sing
it's time now to let that flower bloom
that bud burst forth & blossom
keep the ember burning
which is deep down inside
let it glow bright   ignite
yes   you & I   we together
                              can do it

AsIam Stimulus Prompt

The Task:

- *Write down five random words for each of the letters S T I M U L*
- *Pick any five words you are drawn to of the thirty you now have in front of you*
- *Begin a piece using those five words*

Ann Ryan: her prompt words were

Slurping Turtle Innocent Murphy Unusual Luscious

Murphy the Turtle

Murphy, an unusual looking turtle, sat innocently slurping from his bowl. Licking his lips after the luscious taste, he smirked before stumping back outside.

A gnarled, fallen tree blocked his path on nearing the bottom of the garden. Trying to scamper up, he edged closer to the summit, his paw finding it hard to grasp a foothold. Feeling himself slipping, he tried hard to hold on - one more stretch and he'd make it

Mike Cahn: his prompt words were

Schism Syncopated Mousey Ululation Lilliputian

History Singer's ululation intensified as he started singing from The Second Book of The Song of The Schism.

Straining to hear the words over her wrestling children, Geraldine's mousey face flushed, remembering her naivete in the mid 2020's, when she believed that Blue /Red political differences could be worked out without violence.

Syncopated memories – clunky gas masks knocking into each other as she hugged her fellow protesters, lilliputian dog on a red leash seen beyond the legs of the police.

Flashing Thumping Ringing

A ladybug crawled along her raw zip-tied wrists.

Cian Morey: his prompt words were

Sophoclean Isthmus Mosaic Uncle Lazarus

Uncle Lazarus lived across the isthmus, so we only saw him once a year. Incomparable climactic conditions, a source of fascination for meteorologists worldwide, meant the isthmus was submerged in water for 364 days of the year. So, when the 365th day came and the isthmus shrugged off enough of the tide to be traversable, we always visited Uncle Lazarus.

In the rose garden of my ten-year-old memory, he was a jovial man, with cosy eyes set deep in his friendly cheeks like swaddled babies, and a face with abundant chins. A Sophoclean adage or a jaunty vaudeville lyric could roll off his tongue with equivalent ease, and on special occasions he liked to fashion a nonsense cocktail of the two at once. He was fond of jokes, fonder of gin, and life felt safer in his orbit.

But one year when the isthmus cleared and we crossed to his old familiar house, the person who answered the door and introduced himself as Uncle Lazarus was not him.

Dave Murphy: his prompt words were

Muddled Mouthful Savoury Titillate Insatiable

The Hungry Lunch

The muddled mouthful of sugary, savoury
satisfaction
titillated the tastebuds in tasteful fashion
The unified umami of ultra processed perfection
beat the vegetarian alternative (neglected)
The loveliness of the lip-smack
brought a lecherous lasciviousness to lunching

Insatiable saltiness bubbled joy
The carefree, careless caloried intoxification
smothered the senses
freed the soul
Oh yum, oh nom, oh joy
Let's eat!

Jennifer Kissane: her prompt words were

Sassy Tableau Igloo Military Limbo Usher

Growing Up

Come back! Stay!

Stay? I'm not a dog.

Tossing her flaxen mane, in that sassy way which makes me prickle with envy, Charley leaves her admirer behind.

High heels clipping on uneven footpaths, we wobble to our student digs. A two-bed redbrick residence in Smithfield, sitting in a tableau of equally picturesque houses. Our neighbours work in the tech companies on Grand Canal Dock. They pay exorbitant rents. We, on the other hand, landed this house by fluke.

That is what we admit to anyway.

The ugly truth is that Charley's father buys up houses that the original owners have defaulted on.

The Unfortunate Good Fortune, we've christened our beloved abode, that we are too poor to heat. It is like a faulty igloo most nights. We shiver and wear extra layers until eventually one of us swallows our pride and asks for an advance on our wages, or a sub from our parents. A shared spreadsheet lists our mounting debts. With military precision we catalogue all that is owed, resolving to paying it back and being 'real grown-ups.'

I'm going to make my own choices. I'll not be fettered by their money.

Charley has the luxury of such gilded shackles.

Designer labels, expensive restaurants, and foreign holidays were the foundation of her childhood.

Penneys, pebbledash and Lahinch each August, were the backdrop to my formative years.

Fumbling with the key, the chipped primrose door eventually opens. Charley ushers me in.

I'm soooo cold!

Won't be much warmer in here.

Luke McCormac Parker: his prompt words were

Song Toil Molasses Immune Upheaval

Song drifted over the fields as the 'indentured' labourers of Lady Michaela worked the land.

Toil was good for the soul ,she would say, having done none herself. *Music nourishes the soul,* they would respond when she demanded they work in silence. Her position of power justified by the Atolic Church Scriptures left her with no valid complaint about their work-hymns. Immune to punishment for that act, the men freed their voices as their bodies remained bound.

The small rebellion was a spark of warmth and brotherhood as the autumn fog turned the soil to molasses. But even as they tilled, the true upheaval was in the song, its lyrics and tune hiding plans and the desire for freedom.

Emma Burgess: her prompt words were

spacious mistress music label love

setting all labels aside, Sally launches herself onto his lap, then spilling over
the quandary has always been how to behave in public as someone's mistress
letting the music lead, she wrenches out of a nose dive with a rising leg
happy to call this love, not minor inconvenience, she is smiling wide
ridding herself of weight she relies on him to turn her upright
the click of glasses meeting and she's away
reasons for being alive, name one

Cole Caro: her prompt words were

Stranger incense malice unto lured

Lullabies in the Nighttime

Crusted lips hum deep yet loud against the sea-foam malice, salt spray biting at wild eyes hunkered deep within the cliffside. Above lanterns flicker, villagers drone a sickly ballad as they dredge through the storm to lay the dead to rest.

A dirge accompanied by the foul choke of incense, the stranger splutters, her upward gaze one seeping with a rage only the winds could parry. *Heave* they bellow, toppling the linen wrapped body unto the depths, sea swallowing it whole in one great bite before thrashing an unruly mane against the rocks once more. Never satiated, always hungry - always. They said she lured sailors to their deaths, calloused hands, foot of web, claws dragging, teats sagging, scaling upon the slick sharp drop. Bathing in the bloodshed of the jagged rock, lamenting in lullabies of dead men, gorging on the tears of widows, and of other kin.

Silent she screams. Shrill, agonising. Even sirens weep, her eyes glisten beneath the shadow of grief while she watches her sisters feast. A lover of the land, a monster of the sea; a marriage it was not to be.

Pen and Paper

A u3a Writers Group, formed in 2019 who now meet on Zoom each Thursday , most of whom are based on the Causeway Coast of Northern Ireland

Paul Girvan *~ Collator ~*

As a senior barrister and then as a judge Paul Girvan wrote extensively on legal matters during a long career and he now enjoys the freedom of creative writing particularly poetry which is often inspired by his travels, by nature, by his sense of place, history and time and by his career in law. A keen amateur artist his work is influenced by an artist's eye for colour, form and atmosphere. Paul contributed a prose piece *Affairs of the Heart* to *The Heart of the Matter*, Impspired Press, 2022 and poems to Issue 21of the online magazine and the printed version thereof published by Impspired Press 2023. He was a contributor to the North Coast Writers Anthologies *Woven Words and Spun Tales* and *Woodland Glades and Sea Spray*, Impspired Press, 2022 and 2023 and also to *Writing from the Heart*, collated by Jae Jenkins Scott and Robbie Taylor, Impspired Press 2025

He has published a collection of his poetry *In a Sense,* Impspired Press, 2024.

Agonistes in Gaza

But who are these? For with joint pace I hear
The tread of many feet steering this way;
Perhaps my enemies who come to stare
At my affliction, and perhaps to insult
Their daily practice to afflict me more.
John Milton

That bloodied face I saw on screen

lined eyes   red   oozing   stared

and how they stared   nose flared then tears

rivulets of pain across grey crusted dust

the desiccated grit of wasted years

heart rending sobbing   screams suppressed

no touch of gentle loving hands or hugs

a child mere orphan now   all else is gone

shard shattered turned to wind-blown sand

this child a hostage all alone in seething land.

Wrapped in poisoned spider's web
another girl   a gem just stolen by a thief
a child in terror's grip not loving hands
no more the toys of little girls, kind dolls
soft cuddling of well-loved teddy bears
in dim darkness of a cell she tearful stares
and hears the blast and boom of falling bombs
the thunderous crash of tumbling towers
embittered shouts and roars unkind commands
a hostage child alone in hate-filled lands.

Bovver boys

They put themselves about these bovver boys
invade the pitch come out with golden tousled heads
run out across the field push out the other teams
strut across the grass climb into others' beds
bare teeth serrated sharp these would be lions
glare stare shrug off the weaker wilting ones
they push and shove insert themselves dig in
find regimental strength in numbered ranks
smile laugh and play these strutting dandy boys
ignore the rain   turn faces to the passing sun
turn up in unexpected crannies nooks and gaps
party till they droop and drop   turn all to seed
their glory done grey tops   shaking doddery now
lie about and lounge they pee their bed
await the blowing of the wind or kids
counting the time   the bovver boys take flight
tick tock tick tock put themselves about
again

Scrabbling for Words

Amort in the dreich sleet drizzle

turning almost to a mere smir

my shoes teered by the stag's sharn

I shauchled through the abatis

followed the deer's abanded abature

to arrive at the once fishful pond

ice still afloat on the surface

neustons fixed into frozen shards

I nevelled the ice and plucked

red berries of a drowned holly twig

crimson as the drops of blood

which had dripped like tears

unto the white ground

the trace of a fleeing stag

harried by harder hearts than mine.

Unusual Scrabble words

Amort: depressed

Smir: a fine drizzle

Teered:stained

Sharn: dung

Shauchled: stumbled

Abanded: abandoned

Fishful: full of fish

Neustons: floating organisms

Abatis: a bank of felled trees

Abature: track left by deer

Nevelled: punched

Still Life   Nature Morte

scarlet once exotic those tulips heads erect
stiffened by the pushing of a piercing pin
between the peduncle and the receptacle
onward it comes a creeping discoloration
the glow of a flaming red slow seeps away
the fading of exuberance   a quiet passing
of petals the end foreseen no dusty dust
high hued vestments ash blanched
seductive petals shrinking covers
of a stigma seeking a kiss
ready now detached
they slip and fall
on dead wood
from vase
nature
morte
still
life
aa
aa
aa
aa

Geraldine Fleming

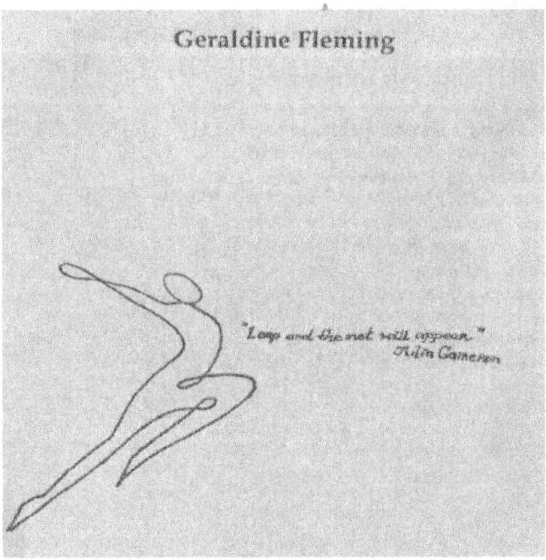

Geraldine Fleming was born and raised in Northern Ireland. After retirement she reconnected with creative writing. Her poetry and prose have appeared in many anthologies and journals. In 2022, two poems were published in Community Arts Partnership Anthology, *Threshold*, and *cartographer* was long listed for the Seamus Heaney Award. The following year a poem was published in the annual CAP anthology, *Compass* and a poem in *Writing from the Heart*, collated by Jae Jenkins Scott and Robbie Taylor, Impspired Press 2025.

She has published a short story collection, *Curiosity*, January 2023 and a poetry collection, *Fractured Echoes,* June 2023, both by Impspired Press.

Summer Solstice on the Mount

balancing on the grassed lip
of this edenic gouge
a shadow-drenched hunter-green bowl
mist agitates between beech & birch
i stare straining above leaf level

first rays of rebirth breach the horizon
kissing the tips of brooding trees
last night

on midsummer's eve
i travelled the path behind my eyes

vestiges of bramble & bracken
fringed by gothic wild garlic
merged with dog roses & ivy

stellar vestigial lines
posed primal imprints
to help meld mind to moment

long ago whispers
inscrutable sounds
bled out their rosetta missive
cauterised through time for a
primed audience

before Stonehenge
before time was gauged

salmon slept & leapt
on this spot
people lived & loved
on this spot
thrived & died
on this spot
invented & invested
on this spot
here we stand ready

from sky to earth
from then to now

the Belt of Venus smears pink light
first rays of rebirth rake the sky
our history is shared

Apophenia

a skewed line hems and haws along
snaking towards check-in and departure
hot breaths exhale a montage of words
snappy snatches snare in dreamcatcher ears
jumbled soundwaves loop their way
jolted synapses livewire then enliven this intrusion
shuffle   kerfuffle   silent speaking
this new language launches coils of allusion
predictive diction without context
inference fashioned to test and tantalise
nuance dances across the mindscape
while sense   of sorts   eventually prevails

Footnote: Apophenia is the tendency to perceive a connection or meaningful pattern between unrelated or random thing

night fear

beyond the artificial buzz of street lights

tar-dark nights recast homely impressions

sweet tap of raindrops prattling along the downpipe

lunge to revamp as thick slick blood soured by the

butcher-sharp knives   mainlining mayhem into the earth

the jacket's jaunty drape   loose-hung   on the door

refashions to a fearsome glaring figure   deep-set eyes

a crooked nose   half-hood hidden consuming the air

hypnotic washing on the line moves from a lazy flap

to reawaken wings of unspeakable night demons

whip-cracking and yowling in their wild ghostly rodeo

playful barks from neighbourhood dogs revise

their tone and timbre fierce fangs froth

demanding the release of the hounds of hell   or else

the swing of branches ease into the swag of shrubs

recast in silhouette the sinister troupe crowd close

and closer still   ready to smother and crush your world

twilight logic garbling clues once solved by daylight

spar in sticky treacle conjuring bone-chilling alternatives

to thwart the release of sleep

Eric Greaves

Soon now, I'll turn and start for home.
And who knows, maybe I'll be singing.

From The Pond by Mary Oliver

Eric Greaves has been writing for approximately five years. A retired financial adviser but active mandolin player, occasional composer and music festival curator.

A member of the Irish Writers Centre he regularly attends Centre courses. In 2022 he received an Irish Government bursary to attend the John Hewitt Summer School where he was enrolled in a creative writing course with author Bernie Magill. Previously a member of the Writing Group *North Coast Writers*, he now attends *Pen and Paper* by Zoom.

His short story *Shades of Jack* was accepted by Impspired for their August 2021 online edition and for their Print Anthology in September 2021.

He is currently editing his historical fiction novel *Covenants*.

Late Frost Remembered

We did not usually walk this wood.
I think this may have been the first.
A white icing remembered because the snowdrops had gone down.
We did not garden then, but knew enough.
Late was lethal.

Crunch on crisp larch and acorns.
Sharp air scorched a sleeping larynx to wake.
A wood caught between seasons can be a wondrous palette.
I gazed in awe and called you back to see a fly agaric.
But even the gods' drink must bow to unseasonal chilling.

But this red and spotted orb sat still in a beech's elbow where it should never belong.
There was magic afoot that day but none as strange as this.
We looked and looked and looked again and fingered this magic fungus to my palm.
What spells muscaria could weave paled beside the sad enchantment revealed that morn.
Frozen huddled ladybirds drawn tight to fight, nature's cold trap sprung.
Alas to no avail...but yet...

Thirty springs and summers on that magic memory lingers late, but not lethal.

The Woodpecker

A wooded walk by the grey lake

now turned to blue by a mantling sky.

A determined three-year-old barrels along the woodland path

leads her beaming ancestor along

this way Grandad this way.

A rattling

tchur tchur tchur

arrests her headlong rush.

The woodpecker bids us both good morrow

but Nature's little warrior is far from charmed.

A strange drilling picks apart the leafy song above the tousled head

all the while the ancient one enthuses in strange tongues.

Do you hear the woodpecker? Do you hear?

No! This strange tattoo is unwelcome in her little world

No grandad!

She runs off smiling now along the wooded path to embrace the water's edge.

Whither the cuckoo thinks the ancient one *he'll arrive in June*

and what of corncrakes on Atlantic eves or a Canada loon?

He rushes forward to the shoreline splasher not a moment too soon

not a moment too soon.

Chaney's Hill

You've come to find the hill from where your ancestors were driven.

You'll come in off the Dublin road to rest under the shadow of Wicklow's old hills. Posters of last Autumn's *Music Under the Mountains* will intrigue... a small place like this to host such artistes. If you are inclined to play some notes or sing with the Hollywood robins and thrushes, your music too will be under the mountains.

For now, stand between the two duelling pubs, facing each other tensely across the cul-de-sac. You may get a sense of 19th century horse fairs, beasts – buyers and sellers long assumed to another place.

Close your eyes and breathe deep and you may get the aroma of dung, tobacco and porter. Listen and you'll hear the tumult of struck bargains, metallic stomp of hooves on cobbles.

You will need to head east into the wood of Johannes Bosco wherein lies your path to Chaney's Hill. But you should first detour west to visit our other holy man, Kevin, lest you leave this place unfairly judged. Where perfidy once stalked, piety walked long years before and since.

So, on by the Castle Bank and into Corrigan's Glen where, if you come at the right time of year, you'll be charmed by the yellow riot of ancient flag irises. You'll pass Kevin's Chair – where you can cure a bad back, and if, you've seen the movie *Michael Collins*, you will recognise the fateful Béal na mBláth.

Now raise your gaze up the cliff face to St Kevin's Cave where he spent penitential days, before decamping for fashionable Glendalough to found a city. In reverie, it's easy to imagine our 6th century hermit and his blackbird gazing down in serene bemusement from his Hollywood redoubt as Liam Neeson draws his last breath below.

Retrace your steps, past Madwoman's Leap and by ancient St Kevin's Church, which these days is a cradle of sweet festival music. On over the Watery Lane and fording the Askinavadda hurtling from the uplands towards Anna Livia. And onwards into the holy wood which holds its secrets tightly. On your left, buzzards rise from beech groves where the granite ruins of Tyrone Lodge lie, razed by the men of '98.

And now you climb steadily to your right through towering beech and holm oak, some descendants of Beresford's planting in the early 1800s.

Beresford, his prolific landscape tree planting of the hills hereabouts, was matched only by his uprooting of so many hapless human weeds.

And as you progress through Kevin and John's sacred old places, you will rest at the Fox Rock where Reynard sat and sneered at Beresford's hounds in their foaming turmoil of pursuit way below.

Your quest is almost done, for sweeping upwards to your right is Chaney Hill cleared by the red-blooded Lord. Hunting parties with untrammelled run over this Wicklow foothill raised grateful bumpers with Beresford of an evening.

Archbishop Robinson of Armagh dithered while dispatches of his nephew Beresford's depredations came to appal the exalted prelate's genteel ears. Finally, the crozier reached south, and thus ended the clearances.

But Chaney's Hill was empty and wild. Your forbears long since trudged away for Liverpool boats.

The Holy City had sought to rescue the Holy Wood, but too late. Acorns of hatred had already fallen to the forest floor.

Robin Holmes

Robin Holmes believes that growing up on a small hill farm in the Mourne Mountains has been a deeply formative experience for his writing. In his poetry he explores themes of the natural world, the life of birds, the changing seasons and man's problematic relationship to the environment. His work has appeared regularly in Bangor Literary Journals and the annual Community Arts Partnership Poetry in Motion Journals. Video recordings of his poems 'Psithurism' and 'Fred Dibnah' are available on the Bangor Literary Journal's YouTube channel. His debut anthology *The Shedding Gate* was published by *Impspired* in April 2024. In the same year Robin was a Winner in the *Impspired Soundwaves Competition.* His poem *The Swans of Gaza* was longlisted for The Seamus Heaney Prize for New Writing in 2024. In this year, 2025, his poem *Ben and Jake* has been included in *Writing from the Heart*, collated by Jae Jenkins Scott and Robbie Taylor, Impspired Press.

Autumn Manna

October, limping towards the year's demise
yet resplendent in russet robes;
you are wedded to the wild, west wind
spreading your bronzed, scorched leaf confetti.
You have enticed my daughters and me
to stray into these ancient woods, and
in trespassing, inherit what is ours.
Our hands delve into the dank mulch
of leaves, to find our treasure;
a storm fall of chestnuts, Autumn Manna.
Some still in the foetal warmth
of spiked kernels, others lying alone,
glistening, staring through buff, bloated eyes.
Obsessively we sift,
with a Klondike zeal,
for their luscious sheen.

Horse chestnuts, like chestnut mares,
rich and redolent;
burnt, burnished, shining
as a dance floor.

Rolling in our palms, as
deep nuggets of Pears Soap;
your browns, your reds,
your polished globes
become our ware.
Our pockets bulge
with your pebbled hulk,
a cunning theft as
we homewards skulk

On Taking Down the Tomato Plants

This is the hour

of unravelling,

of loosening

the ties that bind, from stem and shoot,

mounted, like wedding rings, on a bamboo finger.

In May they were only fist sized fickle plants,

yet with watering, feeding, pruning, they

burgeoned into a veritable rain forest.

Is this the silver lining of that cloud

they call global warming?

By August and September they were bulging,

firm, red snooker balls on a leafy green baize,

week after week they garnished salads and sandwich,

filled the pockets of visiting friends. Yet October sun
has been

an inconstant milk cow, leaving only hard green
marbles

and the thoughts of bitter chutney.

And so this tedious unravelling until all is done, and
secateurs

snip the bottom of stems, a vegetable umbilical cord
it seems:

the plant collapses around me, a puppet with severed
strings;

what remains but a wheelbarrow hearse and
compost bin coffin.

These are the rituals

of a

decaying Autumn.

The Caravaggio of the Carpets

Each morning
a silver, silken, slime trail,
an erratic embroidery
on the kitchen carpet,
announced his intrusion.
But could I find him,
this Midnight Moriarty
determined to taunt me?
'Enough is enough,' I said
as his spirallings,
his Neolithic scratchings,
continued unabated.
And so I placed
a pile of pellets,
a metaldehyde cocktail
to ease his hunger.

Next morning, under the table,
a burst, bloated, mucus membrane,
a black, severed finger,
prostrate and poisoned.
His exit, on a coal shovel hearse,
the black bin his coffin,
disinfectant closed his exhibition.

Afterwards in the silence,
I arrested myself for murder.
Alone in my cell, I began to wonder,
'What would St Francis have done
to this innocent
Caravaggio of The Carpets?

Brenda McAteer

A retired Community Development Worker living in the North Coast town of Portrush, Brenda joined North Coast Writers in 2020. With their help, critiques, stimuli and support, stories and ideas that wander round her head are now appearing on paper.

A flash fiction piece *No Walk No Escape* was performed at Orchard Flash Festival 2021 and can be found on You Tube www.byddielee.com/flash-fiction-armagh. In 2022, a memoir piece *Watch Cup* was published by Northworld NI, and two pieces in 100Voices – NI 100 Years, BCRC. In 2022 her work was also published in the NCW Anthology *Irish Hares and Seahorses* and in the *Love, Loss and Cardiac Issues* both published by Impspired Press as well as in *Writing from the Heart*, collated by Jae Jenkins Scott and Robbie Taylor, Impspired Press, 2025. In 2023 a Flash Fiction piece *Reflections* was performed at Armagh Museum, available on YouTube (link above). She has pieces in the NCW 2023 Anthology *Spun Yarns and Woven Words* published by Impspired Press. In 2024 a Flash Fiction piece *A Walk on the wild Side* was performed as part of the AE festival Armagh, (link above).

Morocco 23

Marrakech
kaleidoscope of colour
souks buzz   sellers hustle
spices saturate   tagines sate
mint tea   poured from on high
welcome smiles
their city

Ourika Valley
Berber cooperatives
rugs   jewellery   argan oil
pots from clay brick kilns
women craft   men market
pride in traditions
their land

Setti Fatma
Kalid hauls us upwards
over narrow bridges   rocks and shale
waterfalls tumble   precipice cafes
his village clings to mountainside
photo of wife and baby
his world

Q
U
A
K
E

magnitude 6.8
calls to Allah rush to the streets
homes villages land shattered
mountain mud brick homes crumble
families villages
obliterated

Kalid
be there
in your world

Snowflake

Curled up in our cloud getting ready to fall. This is it! We've been to snowflake training. So excited I'm not going to be a dread drop of rain, plopping on people. They hate rain.

We're all beautiful, shiny white, six-sided and all different. Just so special. Today is extra special, January 18th – world snowman day – and we've been picked to glide down to earth.

Please, please,

don't let me fall on a road - I'll be slush in seconds
or on water - I'll just melt
or on a roof - no one will see me.

Please, please,

I want to fall in a garden or a field, somewhere a small person can find me and roll me into a snowman. You can last for days if you're part of a snowman.

I'm tingling, we're all bunching closer. Wow! The cloud's burst open. We're falling so slowly, floating, catching each other, blowing apart. I feel light, I'm gliding, it's magical.

Oh, I can see a big blue space with white curls. No, no - not there, that's the sea, I'll be salted away in seconds.

There's a big puff of wind and my cloud mates and I land on rough stuff but it's dry. It's sand, we're on a beach. Lots of other flakes fall too, we cover a big patch of sand. I listen, I hear the waves and squawks of a big-winged thing. I'm just lying here. I want to be useful, to be something.

After a long, long time I hear it, I bristle, get excited. A little person is being pulled over the snow on a bright blue tray thing. She leaps off and charges towards us, screaming and shouting,

Daddy, Daddy, can we build a snowman?

It's a bit cold, Molly, our hands will freeze. Anyway, a snowman on a beach is a bit daft.

Please Dad, please. It'll be special, pleeeaase.

Molly, come over here. I want to be part of a snowman, pleeeasse. I hear her feet crunching towards me, closer, closer - then she stamps just beside me. I'm a jitter with excitement. I'm ready, Molly.

Daddy! Just here, I'll start.

We should have brought your bucket and spade, though in a snow fall I wonder why I didn't think about that, young Molly. Come on help me, let's pile all this together into its body. Getting higher, good girl, it's nearly as tall as you!

Molly, Molly you've flicked past me four times, please pick me up. I'm twinkling as much as I can in the sun, I'm here, just right here.

Right Molly time for the head. I'll start a snowball then you roll it, that's a girl.

Oh, I'm in her hands – don't squeeze so tight, I'm losing my shape. Now I'm going in circles, round and round, I'm dizzy, loads more flakes pressing against me. Wow, this is amazing! I'm part of something.

OK Molly, that's nearly big enough. I'll help you lift it. Excellent. Time for home - my fingers are blue.

Daddy, I have to get shells for eyes and a stone for its nose. You draw a mouth.

Well, that was tickly as the Daddy ran a finger across us. Oh, here comes Molly. She jabs two shells into the head thing and a big piece of stone below. Molly's jumping up and down, singing and laughing. My snowflakes have made her happy. She hugs us. We're happy.

Daddy, I'm going to make it my sandsnowgirl, called Susie. Look, Daddy, I've made sand feet for Susie and sand buttons.

She's dancing round us singing a snowman song. This is what I was made for, so proud.

What's wrong? Molly's crying, water running down her face. She's shouting at Daddy.

No, no, oh Daddy, the tide's coming in. Susie will be taken away just like all my sandcastles. Daddy, we have to move her up the beach, now, now!

Molly, you do know the snow will melt in a few days. Sandsnowgirl can't last forever. Oh, my kitten, come here, don't cry.

Daddy, just move it so I can see Susie in the morning, pleeeasse. Can we put her on my sand tray and pull her back? Can we try, Daddy?

They go away, I'm feeling a bit frightened. What's a tide, why will it take us away? Oh, they're back - what's that?

It's as well I keep a shovel in the car, my poppet. You'll have to help. Hold Susie's head while I slide the shovel under her. Hold tight while I push Susie on to the tray. That's it, strong girl. We'll pull her up towards the sandhills. Slowly, slowly. Oops, eye fallen out. We'll get it in a minute. We're past the tide line here. Sandsnowgirl is safe for tonight.

Molly hugs and kisses Daddy, then us again.

Daddy, take a picture of Susie with me. She's so special. Can I wrap my scarf round Susie to keep her warm?

Just for the picture. Mummy will flatten me if we come back without the new scarf Nanny got you for Christmas.

Molly puts her arms round us. Daddy shouts 'say cheese', and there's a flash. Molly is lifted on Daddy's shoulders. She's shouting and waving at us. She says she'll see us in the morning.

Wow, snowflakes!
We're here 'til the morning.
We're called Susie.
We're in a photo.
We'll last forever!

Safe Places

Fleeing from Jess's house, Teddy just runs. Two tourists leap out of his way as he reaches the craggy path that extends around the clifftop of the narrow inlet, Portcoon Cove. He slows down as he spots the open gash low down on the opposite rock face, a half open eye. Others think it has an evil gaze, not Teddy.

The cove bound by cliffs, one bare basalt, the other has a velvet sheen with grass clinging to the rocks. Midway a trail runs down to the jetty. Teddy slips and slides over wet grass and slimy rocks. The tide is in, he has to climb round a large protruding boulder, then scramble and slither to the fissure, the cave opening. He crawls in, tries not to howl. My safe place, my safe place, he chants to himself as he curls into a foetal position.

Jess just stands, door and mouth wide open. She answered the door, Teddy looked in, uttered a guttural growl, eyes wide and wild, turned shouting - not here, not here, it can't be - and bolts.

Jess had been looking forward to this meeting. Teddy, the boss's son, soon to take over the shop, thawing enough to come for tea and a chat about the future. She was full of ideas to update the store and bring it into the 21st century. Add lines for the increasing number of second homeowners and tourists who now flood the Causeway village. She wanted to add a gift section full of local art, crafts and foods. The shop could go online, have better advertising and ultimately sales.

Arriving in the village six years ago she got a job doing the books and supervising when Pops wasn't in. Pops saw her zeal and had been pushing for her to work closer with Teddy, to take the shop into the future. He had muttered that Teddy needed some support and a bit of her vision.

Ah Jess, from that wee teddy bear of an auburn curly headed, blue-eyed sprite we took in, I've loved and encouraged him. I'm old now, retiring, he can run this business as long as he has background support. You're just right.

Teddy uncurls, eyes still closed, listening. Water whooshing in from the other cave entrance, a huge arch blasted from the open sea. The waves rush towards the lofty forty-foot high cavern he's curled up in. It's dry, it's safe. The sea can enter gently, just quietly lapping, or gush and thrash, sounding like a deafening discordant orchestra, depending on tide and weather. He's sat in this cave to hear and feel it on soft summer days, and through mountainous Atlantic storms. Never afraid, this is his place.

This is where Pops found him all those years ago. A sad and fearful seven, nearly eight-year-old, peering out the cave opening, talking to his fictional mother who didn't shout, cry, or lie comatose on the sofa. This mother, the tall slender rock gazing down at the little rock beside her. Separate but close. Little rock is hidden looking from the cliff top but from the cave eye they are together, both strong, both close. On stormy days when little rock disappears under roaring wild waves, mother rock keeps a steady gaze, protecting him.

Jess frantically phones Pops.

Pops, when I opened the door to Teddy, he looked shocked, made a growling sound, turned and ran off. Didn't even say hello. What's going on?

Jess, exactly where do you live?

You know the big stone farmhouse off the Runkerry Road. Down the track behind it about a quarter of a mile. Converted from a piggery to a worker's cottage. It was nearly derelict when I bought it.

God, oh God Jess not there, I'm on my way, meet me at the back of the Hotel.

Jess flings on a jacket and runs towards the Hotel. Her cottage had been lying empty for years when she bought it. She didn't care. It was hidden, secure and such a bargain. Jess knew she could make it beautiful. She negotiated a piece of land from the farmer and over the years created a pretty cottage garden.

Jess reaches the hotel just in time to see Pops park his van. She rushes over, he leads her to the Cove path.

....

Follow me Jess. Years ago, on my daily walks I kept meeting a little boy wandering round here. A wee waif, but he let me tell him about the Giants Causeway, the hexagonal rocks, the sea life, and mythical stories. I mean, he had to know about Finn McCool, his fights with the Scottish giant, see his shoe and sit on the wishing chair. Hear about the smugglers at this cove and the hermit who lived in the cave and was fed by a seal.

Was that Teddy?

Yes, his mother had moved here when he was three and at first all seemed well. They shopped locally, made friends and Teddy started at the local primary. Then a nasty piece of local shit preyed on her, got her on drugs and things went bad. I'd come up, bring food and try to help. I hadn't seen Teddy for days, so I called at the cottage. She was lying on the floor, covered with his blanket. The smell of sick made me gag. I tried to revive her but, but ....

Was she dead, Pops?

He nodded and shuddered as he relived the horrific scene.

Not a wonder Teddy ran from my door. That poor child, where was he?

When the police arrived, I told them I had to find the boy. I knew he'd be in Portcoon Cave. I brought him back to my home and Wilma and I fought to keep him. Too old to adopt the Welfare said, but they couldn't find other family for him. One social worker could see how Teddy trusted us, and she pushed and pushed until we were allowed to foster him. Made our life, that little boy. We became his Ma and Pops.

They'd reached the midpoint of the cliffs looking over the Cove. Pops led her round to the middle of the western cliff,

See that gash in the rock face, it's one entrance to Portcoon Cave, a mighty structure. I'd taken him in a few times, when he was only six. He loved it. I just knew he'd be there. It's a bit of a clamber to get to it, but the tides going out. Jess, go to him, I'll wait here.

Jess tripped her way down the path, clambered up and over the boulder to see Teddy staring at the tall rock, talking and gesticulating. She didn't want to intrude but lost her footing and slid towards the cave mouth, shrieking.

Twice in one day, you've put the fear of God in me Jess. What the hell are you doing here?

Pops sent me, he said you'd be in this cave. I'm mortified Teddy. I didn't know you lived at my cottage, and your poor Mum passed away there. I'm so, so sorry. It was derelict, cheap and I was desperate to get away from Belfast. I'd escaped an abusive relationship, so I asked no questions and kept a distance from the locals. I know they think I'm a stuck-up cow. I just rely on Pops and you. Who were you talking too?

Don't laugh, I speak to that tall rock when I come here. I asked what I should do, who could I turn to - when you dramatically dropped by.

They scramble in. Jess is amazed how bright it is. Teddy pulls her into where the rock shelf drops. Open to the sea on one side, she clings to him as the water rolls up towards them but cries out in awe when she turns to see the high cavern to the right.

Pops said it was a mighty structure, wow.

Some call it a Gothic Cathedral. The sea rarely reaches the back of the cavern. Its dry and still, even when all around is stormy. My safe place.

They hear Pops call from the cove opening. Teddy charges at him shouting, crying out,

Pops you could have been hurt, fallen, killed. Another safe place would have been destroyed. Seeing the old cottage just brought such back dreadful memories, feelings. Pops, I could never ask but I always thought Mum choked on the cereal I made her eat before I went to bed. Pops - did I kill her?

Pops grabs him, signals to Jess, who puts an arm round him too.

No, no, no son, why didn't you ask years ago. Drugs killed her, a dirty mix, that rat did time for it. Nothing, absolutely nothing to do with you. You covered her with your blanket, you cared.

They sat in a huddle for a while, Teddy quietly keening. Pops and Jess held him tight. Teddy stares at mother rock. He silently asks, should he accept support from Jess? Little rock suddenly glows as a shaft of sunlight illuminates it.

Teddy gasps, grabs Jess's hand and nods to mother rock.

Sue Steging

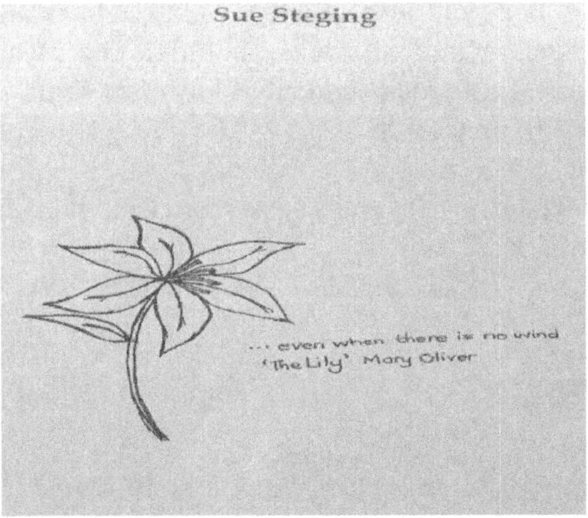

Sue's work has been published in on-line journals, in magazines, and anthologies. Readings can be found on the YouTube channels of The Bangor Literary Journal, Issue 11 and the Community Arts Partnership anthologies, *Heartland* (2021) and *Threshold* (2022) where her poems, *The Goldfinch* and *a naming of* parts were longlisted for the Seamus Heaney Award for New Writing. In 2023 she received the award for her poem, *Four Stories About (The Same) Crows.* In 2024 Sue was a Winner in the *Impspired Soundwaves Competition.* This year, 2025, her poem *From Winter to Spring* has been included in *Writing from the Heart*, collated by Jae Jenkins Scott and Robbie Taylor, Impspired Press.

your gate will be shown...

if I were a poet I would hear
our still sad music through the noise
the circling of conditioned air
the shops that try
to ease our worries with a toy
the called-out confirmation
of a misheard name   scribbled
on a climate-heating one-use cup
the final calls for passengers who haven't learned
you have to watch to know the gate is shown
the ticking of predictive text   oh no
I meant to write of charms not harms
you called when I was deafened by the din
and now I see the gate has closed

unmoored

The ridges here recall the times when
life was only single-celled or shelled,
before we found our way to land.
Sea cliffs rise; seem pathed and paved,
as shadows shape a city in white stone.
Wild Sea Pink masquerades as silk,
a pennant laid against the green,
as though to welcome us back home.

A splash of sun. The tableau fades.
A taste of ice drifts from the north,
where islands seem like us, unmoored,
beneath the grey unfathomed skies.
We float on Kraken's deepest seas,
and dare to dream he will not wake

afforesting

some close at hand

still green

still capped

some spread

by wind   by birds   by squirrels or

the draught of passing cars

some half-eaten   dropped mid-flight

some cracked by tractor wheels

some whole

cupules that encode a tree

from root tip winter larders to bright leaves

they count the hours

keep watch until the sun calls time

to let the gene pools fall

this year's mast is generous

my gathering's industrious

I see a forest waiting

patient

in my hands

I'll pass some on

friends have a field to fill

afforesting

an atom of atonement

for the damage we have done

these others I'll keep close

in soft and secret pockets

save them for a second drop

near home

where those who can't tell weed from tree

won't see

Rhona Stephens

Born in Northern Ireland, Rhona Stephens divides her time between Scotland's Royal Deeside and Ireland's Causeway Coast. She enjoys writing poetry and prose, drawing inspiration from the natural world and her Christian faith. In 2023, she was short listed for the *Wells Festival of Literature Open Poetry Competition* and long listed for *The Rialto Nature and Place Poetry Competition.* Her work has appeared in *Irish Hares and Seahorses* and *Love, Loss and Cardiac Matters*, published by Impspired Press, 2022; in *Spun Yarns and Woven Words*, Impspired Press, 2023; in *Sea Spray and Woodland Glades*, Impspired Press, 2024; on *Retreat West* website and in *Writing from the Heart*, collated by Jae Jenkins Scott and Robbie Taylor, Impspired Press, 2025. Her poems for children have appeared in *The Toy* magazine and on *Tyger Tyger, Parakeet, The Dirigible Balloon* and *Charles Causley Trust* website.

Moments of Surprise

What we hope for is the moment of surprise.

Pádraig Ó'Tuama

Surprise can be a lovely thing
brought safe to birth with joy,
or something that unravels us
and threatens to destroy.
When words surprise as weapons and our
language fuels hate,
no power on earth can bring goodwill,
no deed can compensate.

The best of all surprises comes
when that which we expect
is overturned by kindness through

fresh efforts to connect.

With gentle dialogue and grace,

truth, hope and trust increase.

A nascent language of surprise

can sow a seed of peace.

Oh Lord, surprise us. Give us words

that speak to restoration.

A world without surprises is

a world of devastation.

Surprise can save and make us -

can make the foolish wise,

so help us bring this troubled world

sweet moments of surprise.

Gracious words are like a honeycomb, sweetness to the soul and health to the body.

Proverbs 16:24

Grace Note

Lark in the clear air, she says.

Listen. See? Like this.

She draws the bow across the string.

A strong downbeat, a fold and turn,

a sonorous twist and flare.

Rosin rising like incense, I hear

not open A, nor sweet seduction

in a timely bow-tip triplet,

nor the flow of Celtic melody

passed on and down. I hear a lark,

a lark in the clear air,

and my spirit soars.

Kelly's Hill

Though I spent the whole afternoon walking in the wood, still I cannot relax and find myself unable to sleep. A restless wind tip-taps bare twigs of the old apple tree against my bedroom window and I rise, slip on a cosy gown and fold myself into the window seat. It is so dark outside that the outline of the tree is obscured until a fractured moon is released from behind a cloud. Momentarily, it scatters sufficient light for me to make out the apple tree and beyond, as far as Kelly's Hill.

Winter light is precious and I made the most of it today, leaving a dozen duties unfinished as I headed out after lunch. Light was combing the hills, the sun already dipping towards the horizon, though it was still early in the afternoon.

Drawing close to the scatter of birch trees that marked the entrance to the woods, I noticed that they, too, were laced with light, bare limbs silvered by the sun. Tugs of sheep's wool were caught in the barbed wire round the edge of the adjoining field, though the sheep were no longer there. I stopped a moment by the gate to Barnaby's Field, enveloping myself in the scene, with the greedy appreciation of one who knows it may soon be gone forever.

A deftly ploughed field is a thing of beauty. Arrow straight rows, rich soil turned heavenward, furrows stretching to the horizon. As my eye traced the fold and fall of the drills, I saw him. Hugging the hedge, a fox, already lean, though we have not yet turned the calendar on December. He jogged the length of the field before making an abrupt turn and disappearing from view between the trees. Perhaps we'll meet later, I thought, as I, too, joined the path that would take me deep into the beating heart of the woods.

It seemed to me that they knew, these slim birch and alder and shadowed pine, knew their future was uncertain. They leaned toward me, impressing upon me their stature, their significance. Anchors for the soil, wombs and nurseries, a refuge to some, a home to many, a joy to all. What a consolation of bark, boughs and stately spires, quiet globes of lichen bracketing low branches and birds, birds, birds everywhere, flitting and feasting on an early supper before sundown.

And then, the crowning glory of the afternoon. A rare sighting of a pine marten, arrested on a fallen log, one paw suspended, dark against its creamy bib, watching me with a hushed boldness that belied its reputation as a shy creature. We held each other's gaze for several minutes and it was I who moved off, not he. A benediction of beauty and song and life all around me. See, everything seemed to say, this, all of this, will be lost. I felt an ache rise from my chest to my throat.

Leaving pines and pine marten behind, I climbed to the summit of the hill, past the ruins of Kelly's cottage and, with winter's eye upon me, considered how blessed I was to be there. Not until the shadows lengthened and the woods took on the shades of evening did I head home.

***

Here, in the bedroom window seat, the ache settles again in my throat, the sweetness of the afternoon soured by thoughts of *Breckenridge & Taylor Property Developers*. Memories of last night's meeting in the village hall oppress me.

There was standing room only for those of us who squeezed in after work or after putting children to bed. And Jerry Breckenridge on his feet, placating uneasy villagers with platitudes, with promises of pathways here and play areas there, a bus stop and speedy access to the motorway to Belfast by way of a new roundabout - in the middle of the ploughed field the fox had skirted this afternoon. *Exceptional Design, Quality Homes, Affordable Prices,* he guaranteed. Everything constructed with *award-winning sensitivity to the local environment* - though yes, he acknowledged, the lower slopes of Kelly's Hill would have to be cleared.

"But I'd just like to remind everyone, so I would, " he continued, honeying his tones, "yous are in desperate need of housing in this area. We're building these houses for your families - your children, your... your Daddies and Grannies, Great-Aunts. They'd love to see out their days in the place they were born, so they would."

I'm not sure who was most surprised by what happened next: Jerry Breckenridge, my village friends, or myself. With a boldness as uncharacteristic of me as of the pine marten I met today, I called from the back of the hall.

"Mr Breckenridge? Could I just remind *you* that your plans are for *luxury dwellings*, with a token row of four so-called *affordable homes.* And nothing, nothing at all suitable for our Grannies and Great-Aunts..."

"And you are?" Mr Breckenridge interrupted.

"Brianna Meddowes."

"Well, Brianna," he continued, all affability and openness, "Like I said, yous are desperately in need of housing here..."

As he paused for breath, I took the opportunity to pick up where he left off.

"No-one is disputing the need for housing. Yes, we want, we need local homes for local people, but the houses you want to build won't fall within our budgets. There's not one person in this village who could afford them."

Nods of assent and murmurs of agreement gave way as applause spread round the hall.

"And another thing," I continued, when a fresh silence fell. "I've had a close look at your plans. You've done as little as legally possible to minimise environmental impact and accommodate local wildlife. Have you actually walked round the area you propose to develop? Have you been up Kelly's Hill? Have you taken a walk through the woods you intend to *make a way through*? You may be ticking boxes for the council and planners, but you're not ticking our boxes, Mr Breckenridge. You're not listening *to* us, you're not building *for* us. "

His words lit a fire in me from kindling I was not even aware I had laid. I pressed my views home. At some length. And when I finished, well, Mr Jerry Breckenridge brought the meeting to as speedy a close as decency allowed, said he'd be in touch and headed home. As did I. Then, first thing this morning, my mobile rang and the chair of the community action committee asked me to head up an official protest group. I declined, of course. Told him I'm neither campaigner, public speaker, nor eco warrior. But Bernie McGee would have none of it.

"Have a think about it, Brianna. Sure there's no great rush. Take your time. I'll give you a call at the beginning of next week. And remember, we'll all work with you. You won't be on your own. I believe - and I'm not the only one who thinks it, so I'm not - I believe that with you at the helm, we have a good chance of sending Jerry Breckenridge back down the motorway. And not by way of a new roundabout."

***

All morning, I had not been able to get Bernie's call out of my head. All afternoon, too, as I made my way through the woods. And now, here I am, leaning my head against the window frame, hands clasped around my knees, making a litany of names of trees and flowers and wild things. I remember the party of toadstools I came across between the toes of a birch. I remember the pine marten speaking a thousand words in its silence. And I imagine a future in which the sweetest of seasons would bear the sharpness of grief for all that we lost because... Because...silence can condemn as well as speak. My thoughts are still meandering as the moon breaks free from cloud cover again, pooling light on the garden, the meadow, the distant contours of Kelly's Hill.

It is unconscionable that Breckenridge and Taylor should have their way, unopposed. My mind is made up. I'll phone Bernie tomorrow. Laying my gown over the back of a chair, I return to bed, confident that sleep will come quickly now.

****

Sanderlings

A Writers Group founded in 2022 who meet weekly in Portstewart, Northern Ireland

A Sanderling: a small wading bird who forages for nourishment along the edge of the sea

Sinead Coxhill

Having grown up on a farm in Northern Ireland, Sinead Coxhill studied English at Queen's University Belfast before moving to England. Returning to Northern Ireland from a smallholding in Suffolk in 2013, she settled in the north coast town of Portrush, writing poetry and in 2014, joining Portrush Writers and later, North Coast Writers.

Touring parts of England in 2018 performing at open mic events, 2019, she performed at the Red Sails and Stendhal Festivals in Northern Ireland, and in 2022 at the Abbey Lane Theatre, Armagh in Northern Ireland.

Her poems have been published in 10 anthologies : *Spindrift*, Portrush Writers, 2018, the Community Arts Partnership anthology *Heartland*, 2020, *Reeling In*, Portrush Writers, 2021, *Irish Hares and Seahorses*, a North Coast Writers anthology, Impspired Press, 2022, *Across the Threshold*, a pamphlet and companion publication to the Community Arts Partnership's Threshold anthology, 2022, *Love Loss and Cardiac Matters* , Impspired Press, 2022, *Compass*, a Community Arts Partnership anthology, 2023 *Spun Yarns and Woven Words*, Impspired Press, 2023, *Sea Spray & Woodland Glades,* Impspired Press, 2024, *Writing from the Heart*. Impspired Poets on Writing, collected by Jae Jenkins Scott and Robbie Taylor, Impsired Press 2025

In August 2023 her debut Poetry Collection, *Menopausal Mermaids & Life Lines* was published by Impspired Press

Grain of Sand

I carry you with me

you are a grain of sand
waves washing over me
seaweed tangling round my feet

you are the power of surfers
a concentration of castle builders
a girl whizzing past on a scooter

you are cows calling to their calves
bull strutting proud
a fox in the hen house

you are a ladybird flexing its wings
a nettle which stings my hand
wind-blown dandelion seed on my face

you are a blizzard obstructing everything
a chink of light as darkness disappears
nebulous rainbow, a half arc missing

you are all places,
all times, all seasons,
you are the world

I carry you with me

Tea Break

The proprietor's eyes took in her stained coat.

'I'm meeting a friend. I'll wait til she comes so we can order together.'

Clarice tucked herself away in the corner on the lumpy two-seater next to the children's toys, guessing it wouldn't be a popular time for mums and toddlers. This gave her the opportunity to be out of the way, watching the comings and goings with interest.

An obese, sweaty man sat down to a huge fry of double helpings.

He's asking for a heart attack if he doesn't cut down.

An elderly couple had coffees with pain au chocolat and millionaire's shortbread. She marvelled that anyone could have such a sweet tooth. Seated together were a middle-aged woman and a girl who looked about fifteen. The woman tried to chat to the teenager who responded by scrolling down her phone. Exuding world weariness, even the mobile had limited attraction for her.

Gazing around, the décor was tired but homely. It had been some time since her last visit here. Keeping moving from café to café was her policy. A return would only be made when she thought her face would be forgotten. People watching was a favourite pastime, thinking of how much she'd like to write things down, turn them into stories. She'd been musing for nearly an hour when the proprietor approached her.

*'Your **friend** hasn't arrived.'* He emphasised the word ***friend.***

'She must be running late.' Clarice longed for a coffee but only had enough money for a tea.

'I'll have a tea while I wait for her'.

He rolled his eyes. The tea would buy her some time. At 4.00pm staff began wiping down tables and stacking chairs. She paid for her tea and left.

Hunching up against the rain, she crossed Bluebell Drive, made her way down Peony Road. The last house was an eye sore. Jagged broken windows leered, like a mouth of rotting teeth. Making her way round the back, checking for observers, she slipped through the back door.

The house smelt damp, wind howling through the broken windows, offering no warmth but was some sort of protection from a life on the streets. It was only a matter of time before local kids or street drinkers discovered it. The future couldn't be a consideration. There was only today.

Taking off her coat, wrapping herself in a tattered blanket, she climbed into her sleeping bag, squirreling down inside. It hadn't been a bad day, she mused, remembering the people she'd watched in the café. She had a few ideas for stories.

Someday, someday. She smiled.

Candles

bringing them to life

a single match

like Cinderella enchanted

by her fairy godmother

flames stretch heavenward

pirouetting, burnishing copper scuttle

curtseying, leaping

bowing to each other

holding a firelight communion

they burn with an intensity

self consuming

as an ardent artist or poet

they mesmerise, hypnotise
share our joys and sorrows
celebration and prayer
pure perfumes released

lavender, rose, cinnamon
a cornucopia of scents
to delight the senses
and enfold the heart

I wish not to extinguish
your dancing brightness
but the call of the world
is waiting to be answered

Hope

Cutting had been her means of expressing distress.

Daisy sat before her counsellor confessing how she'd tried to harm herself that year. Images of Poppy, a lively three-year-old, mischievous, loving, wholly lovable played in front of her eyes. She smiled a fleeting smile before the image of her little sister, limp and lifeless, seared itself on her senses. The scorching heat of the word 'Meningitis' burnt through her brain.

With affection neighbours had referred to Poppy as 'a late one'. At nineteen Daisy was sixteen years older.

Poppy had been her shadow, hanging on her every word, loving being picked up and twirled around, seeking cuddles and always full of giggles.

The loss of Poppy was a hammer blow to her heart. Sometimes Daisy felt it would kill her. At times she didn't care if it did. Often at night time, ambushed with memories of those last desperate days, her throat constricted with the same fear which had gripped her then.

Two months before Poppy's death, Daisy had passed her exams as a Nursery Nurse. She applied to work in the local nursery and been accepted. Her starting date would have been the day of Poppy's funeral.

Three years on from that day the manager of the nursery telephoned her about a vacant post. Daisy couldn't believe anyone could be so insensitive, but another part of her responded to the gentleness of the manager's voice. She consented to a meeting. It was suggested that Daisy give the job a two week trial period. They agreed that she would observe, not interact with the children.

She was surprised at how much she enjoyed watching the children playing together. On her eighth day a little girl with a solemn gaze approached her. Daisy allowed herself to be led to the table with the play doh.

Denise Ellis

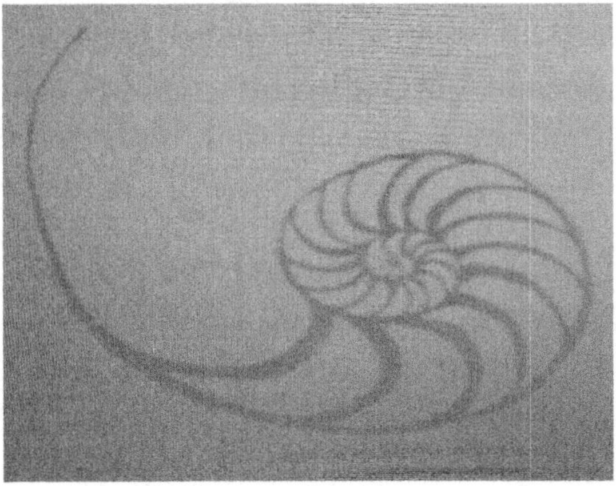

Having lived and worked on the North Coast of Northern Ireland for thirty-five years, Denise presently lives in the seaside town of Portstewart. Since joining Sanderlings Creative Writing Group in the Spring of 2023, and encouraged by the other Group Members, she has found herself writing ever since. Always interested in the natural world, especially in birds, Nature and the stunning landscape where she lives influence inspires her writing. Five of her pieces featured in the Anthology *Seaspray and Woodland Glades*, Impspired, 2024. Her poem *Devil Birds* can be seen in *Writing from the Heart*, collated by Jae Jenkins Scott and Robbie Taylor, Impspired Press 2025

Tempus Fugit

Tick tick tick   louder faster   running on

running out   seasons change

fleet as memory

spring tide

full moon

wax

wane

long hot

Summer not   tepid

dank winter   no crisp   deep

or even cold   here I sit   perpetual

Autumn   mystified melancholic wistfulness

Three Birds

Lapwing

Iridescent child
fledged the humble scrape to soar
swerve sustain your own

Wren

Pert Lothario
Springs transcendent Aria
Mythic king of birds

Curlew

Melancholy Wraith
Curlew curfew curlee cries
foretell near demise

Blest

Basalt shoulders heft a laden sky
Lir presides from a lofty helm over
a golden hoard
his kingdom near

Cocooned in a nimbus shroud
indolent sun   declines to warm
the solemn progress
far below

Treading an ancient route
        bordering a steel-grey lough
                wintering swans whoop
                        a sonorous lullaby
                                Curlews lament
                                        those gone before

Last walk along a village street
doors open   heads bow
in reverence
Remembrance

Upwards   up where forebears lie
Words of comfort   blessings
said as light beams through
to gentle her eternal bed

Yvonne Hamilton

Are you sitting comfortably?

A retired primary school teacher living in the seaside town of Portstewart in Northern Ireland, Yvonne Hamilton has been a member of a writing group for three years. She started to write when forced to retire from a small amateur orchestra as poor night vision had made it unsafe for her to travel to rehearsals. That gave her the time - her dogs gave inspiration. In 2023 her first book, *Fetch*, a book of short dog stories, was published by *Impspired Press*. Other pieces were published in the Anthologies, *Love Loss and Cardiac Issues*, 2022, *Spun Yarns and Woven Words*, 2023, and *Woodland Glades and Sea Spray*, 2024 all published by *Impspired Press*. In 2022 Yvonne read her own work at a Portstewart Library, Northern Ireland as part of the *Aging Gracefull*y Initiative. Selections from *Spun Yarns and Woven Words* and *Fetch* were performed at St Paul's Tuesday Club, in Articlave, Northern Ireland, in June 2023.

Emma's Letter

The letter was finished. She wrote once or twice every week, knowing that the letters meant so much to him. Just one quick read through before she posted it.

My Darling *14th August 1978*

We miss you all the time and talk about you every day.

I know that you're disappointed to be missing Peter's birthday, but we have come up with a solution. He'll be given the present from you on his birthday (it's some new Dinkie cars and a garage safely hidden in your mum's house) and the party will be when you come home. I don't believe that two-year-old boys rate parties as long as the presents appear!

We walked round to visit your Mum and Dad this morning (they are both in good form - sending you their love as usual). It rained while we were there so, on the way back, all the cracks, holes and hollows in the footpath were filled with water. We played a game of jumping over the puddles till Peter accidently jumped into one. He stood there for a moment looking in amazement at the remains of the puddle, and then at me, and then he laughed. I could see the wheels turning, the fun bubbling, knew what was coming. Your son jumped in every puddle for the rest of the way so that we both arrived home soaked to the knees.

He's going to a party tomorrow and the shoes will never be dry in time so I decided to buy him a pair of wellingtons that he can wear to the party, changing to his slippers when he arrives. So, after lunch it was off to the shoe shop - in slippers.

Rosemary was working there and produced two pairs of boots: a black pair and a green pair – both good male wellington colours – both rejected. She retired to the store again to appear with a bright red pair. Peter's face lit up and I sent up a silent prayer that they'd fit.

We were the only customers in the shop and, as she sat on the stool to put on the second boot, Rosemary asked about you in a voice barely above a whisper. I said you were in Germany. I know that is not where you are, but I can't face the look of sympathy if I tell the truth. I know that her son had been posted to Northern Ireland. As I also knew that she didn't raise her eyes from the red boots for fear the tears of worry and dread which had gathered in her eyes would spill over.

I put my hand gently on her shoulder.

Peter broke the spell. He slid from the chair and clumped over to the mirror. "My boots!" he said to his reflection.

Rosemary turned away to wrap up the slippers. We both knew that they would not go back on. The red boots marched home.

I must hurry so I don't miss the post. Do stay safe and keep writing. I read Peter something from your letters each night after his story, so he goes to sleep thinking of you. And so do I.

Love always from both of us,

Alice XXX

She addressed the envelope, sealing the letter inside before fixing the stamp. She would have time to catch the post before Peter's bedtime.

"Come on and we'll post the letter to Dad. You can pop it into the post box. You'll soon be tall enough to reach the opening by yourself."

He always held her hand while she carried the letter until they reached the post box. Then she would lift him up to put the letter in. He was the Letterbox Man.

"Teddy come too," he shouted. As he ran to fetch Teddy Alice opened the door to find a man and a woman approaching her up the path.

She didn't recognise them.

They were strangers.

They didn't belong.

Both smart.

She, in her dark suit, with her hair in a neat bun at the back of her neck and her sensible shoes.

He with the white shirt tidy tie expensive suit brightly polished shoes and short trim hair-cut

both in suits.

They were not in uniform.

He displayed an identification card. “Mrs Rothwell? Major Armstrong and Sergeant Jones. May we come in?”

His lips continued to move but she heard nothing of what was being said. All drowned out by the roaring in her ears as she slid down the wall.

The letter fell from her fingers and fluttered to the floor.

Wolf's Letter

Hi Brother,

If you could see me now. What a day. You wouldn't believe it. And it's not over yet! Would love to be able to tell you about it, wolf to wolf, but this letter will have to do.

It all began on my usual circuit marking my territory. I arrived at our message tree, (plenty of messages but none from you, I noticed) was sniffing round it when I heard a sound. I stood still, pricked up my ears, lifted my nose into the wind. I sniffed. Yes. Human. Female. Young. Sweeeet. I could hear that she was singing. A song about a big surprise in the woods for some bears. Huh!

I trotted round the message tree on to the path. When she turned the corner I was standing in front of her. Not too near. She stopped singing, stood still. She was small and wrapped up in something red - my favourite colour - and she held a basket in one paw. I have always marvelled at their ability to do that - the humans, you know, walking on their hind legs. I know it makes them slow, but it does free up a paw or two for carrying things. I can't tell you the number of times I have caught a fly in my throat when I was carrying something in my mouth. If you happen to catch a wasp or a bee ... well, you can be in trouble!

But on with the story. Where was I? Let me see .... a basket in one paw. Ah yes. She stopped. I wagged my tail. They seem to like that. She smiled and stepped nearer. I smiled - not the wide, teeth-glittering, mouth-slobbering leer that the sight of her inspired. A small, timid, friendly lift at the corners of my mouth. I fought against the curl of my lips that could so easily turn into a snarl. She moved nearer, started to talk. I kept my tail wagging gently and tried to sift through the avalanche of words which poured out of her little pink mouth as she inched nearer. Granny Sick Cakes Visit Woods Strangers Cottage Lake. Above this I heard the clunk of an axe.

Suddenly I could smell another human. Near. Too near. I turned from her, trotted off into the trees. I knew where she was going.

The door was unlocked when I arrived at the cottage by the lake – the Granny in bed. I .... think she might have died when I jumped on the bed. Anyway, when she stopped screaming I stuffed her into the wardrobe.

So here I sit; tucked up in a Granny bed; wearing a long sleeved high necked flowery Granny nightdress; a pair of Granny glasses on my nose; a frilly Granny cap hiding my ears. Waiting.

I hear her singing now. Still about the bears who were to be surprised in the woods. I can smell her. She is at the door. I am ready.

I'll finish this letter later - much later.

I like to take a nap after dinner.

Pam Leetch

Born and raised in Ballymena, Northern Ireland, Pamela Leetch spent her adult working life in England. During that time, she maintained her roots through family bonds and an enduring love for her birthplace. Now returned to live in Portstewart, Northern Ireland, scene of many a happy holiday, she is a member of the Sanderlings Creative Writing Group in which she has begun to write about her roots and explore her love of the written word in all its forms. Her work featured in *Seaspray and Woodland Glades*, a North Coast Writers Anthology, 2024, and a prose piece *Your feet will take you there* was included in *Writing from the Heart*, collated by Jae Jenkins Scott and Robbie Taylor, 2025, both published by Impspired Press.

drive

Once upon a time and long long ago there was

a long straight road   empty of people   one car only   far far away

Sunday afternoon going home   seaside sun   ice cream treat

that one car approaching   erratic weaving

W a t c h

a single word shrieking   love   care   the future

hand touching arm   brakes   screech

S t o p

five seconds after impact her world explodes

glass flying   metal crumpling   then silence

S u s p e n d e d

i n

m i d- a I r

no seat belts   too long ago   free fall

time-black   after-shock   roadside

B r e a k d o w n

and now she drives those country roads

seeking   soulless   for the place where those cars came together

crashed   imploded   changed everything in five seconds

as the map of her world died   the perfect circle closed for her

and those who took their final breaths

Alive

I am a kitchen cupboard door, one of many. My task is to house and protect the good dinner plates although I often find that I am required to look after other things as well. Quite a few changes have taken place for me, but I remain basically as I have always been, a sturdy wooden door with a practical use and a practical outlook on life.

My colour changes every couple of years in Spring time when the kitchen is cleared of the winter dust and debris. The Woman gives me a clean and a rubdown with something quite rough which can feel uncomfortable. It's worth it, though, for the soothing feel which follows of fresh liquid cooling energising. The Woman smiles when she sees the colour emerging on my surface. I can't see it myself but I can see the others so I suppose I must look similar. This year we looked like the sky outside. My view through the window.

The Woman appears in front of me as if from nowhere. I cannot see round corners. I can only see what is in front of me. Mostly the legs which walk around me talking doing things which create smells. The smells have to be strong before I can identify them but, when I do, I know I will soon be opened up to disgorge my hidden treasures. Darkness becomes light. My other face has the chance to see to observe the world outside. I, on the other hand, am forced to endure a moment or two of intimacy with my next-door neighbour. Somehow we manage to exchange greetings then I swing back into my rightful place. My alternate face is more familiar with that of the Woman as she bends to take out the plates, whereas I mostly see just her feet and legs.

My most constant companion in this world of mine is the cat who sees me when he enters the kitchen, comes to rub himself against my smooth surface in a most affectionate manner.

My inner core is of strong and rough wood repelling the ravages of time and wear. My surface is wipe-clean porous and can be changed with ease according to another's will. I am okay with this as long as no one interferes with that inner core.

I was once removed from my body for some work to be done. I made it difficult for them to reattach me as I felt they were heavy handed in their dealings with me. I swelled up. I bloated to one side. I refused to fit back into the space that was mine.

They responded by shaving a bit off me. I didn't like that one bit. By tacit mutual consent we have not done that again.

Summer Stroll

A frog tiptoes across a dark forgotten corner of the garden. Up on his hind legs he emerges from the lush, damp grass. Dressed in green frockcoat and yellow breeches he is a fine figure of a frog. Passing by a patch of chartreuse-flowered lady's mantle he pauses to listen to their pleasant melody. Their song attracts many varieties of butterfly. This pleases the frog who picks up the melody, dances onward.

A whirr of owlet's wings delivers a faint scent of garlic to the warm sunlit air. The frog manages to avoid the houndstongue, lolling in an adolescent way across his path, the hairy tentacles threatening to disturb his nonchalant afternoon stroll. He jumps athletically over it.

The frustrated yapping follows him as he continues onward, towards his chosen destination, the garden pond.

Footnote:The stimulus for this piece was to pick four random references from Act IV Scene 1 of Shakespeare's Macbeth, spoken by the Three Witches. Shakespeare used common everyday plants and seeds but gave them magical properties. I was allocated toe of frog (bulbous buttercup); tongue of dog (houndstongue, a highly toxic plant featuring long, hairy stalks); owlet's wing (garlic or ginger plants) and tiger's chaudron (lady's mantle).

Milliken, Jimmy

lost verses …

… forgotten fragments

Having grown up in Northern Ireland Jimmy Milliken spent much of his adult life in the Shetland Islands, but currently lives near Ballycastle on the north coast of Ireland. He has twice been shortlisted for the *Seamus Heaney Poetry Award*; in 2018 for his poem *Mercy Killing* and in 2020 for *Lichen*. His poem *The Butt* was longlisted for the 2019 Bangor Literary Journal Poetry Competition. Another poem *Colloquy* was shortlisted for the *2020 Bangor Literary Journal 40 Words Competition* and appears on YouTube. He has performed his poetry at various showcase events and readings throughout Ireland, including at The Seamus Heaney Homeplace in Bellaghy, in Portstewart, Ballymoney, Ballycastle, Limavady and most notably on a mountain top in Connemara.

His first poetry collection, *Cracking the Air*, was published by *Impspired* in 2022. Further poems have featured in five anthologies published by *Impspired*, a chapbook *Autumn Fragments* published by Seamus Heaney Homeplace, and in every annual Community Arts Partnership Anthology published between 2016 and 2023. In October 2023 he won the inaugural *Soundwaves Competition prize* for Best Performance Piece for his poem *walking the strand.*

lost verses

1.

in a glass bottle discarded on the ebb

a frayed page from your notepad
& scribbled words from
a song
a poem
in your quivering hand

a ragged feather from a raven's wing
found on the sand

for luck   a groatie buckie

whiffs of smoke
from the driftwood fire
& the spliff

the stopper screwed tight

& tossed into the midnight tide

2.

sounds   like he'd come out of the earth
dank & mossy   between rocks & trees
playing them pipes   off-beat rhythm
throb of taut skins   a windy reed
frog on a lily pad   elf dance   hop head
song of a timber wolf   full moon howling
Lakota spirit chant   tin can music
& all the time   man   he was rocking

hair & beard   wild & flowing
Viking horns   hearing never seeing
blind   man   blind   nothing in his eyes
but   the white   white   whiteness
& a look on his face   like he was watching
the other side of the sky

3.

memory rears
feedback from a battered guitar
fuzz & haze

screech of neurons
bleeding notes the colour of
rage & tears
warp   snort   distort   smoke
a beach black thing

iridescence seeps

screech of feedback blares

haze & fuzz   a smear of sunset
embers   flare   swallow   choke
& your words   dissipate
in the campfire's smoke

4.

she is down by the water today   the grey lady
standing in the shrieking stillness
of withered grasses

looking out   across forgotten distances
beyond the islet   beyond the lake
to a further shore

her hair   a beacon   bundled in an auburn bun
though some tresses
neglected   fall free

by her side   a wanderer who moves
between the realms of
earth   water   sky

the marsh wader   silver   grey

here in this liminal space
where the realms merge

what might he portend
standing   vigilant
motionless

it is late   wisps of mist float on the waters
distorting   obscuring
what might have been

5.

bleached by weathers   faded now
but the memory of the colours remains
merging into this soft warmth

how many years since she put
these yarns together
on a hand-framed machine

drawing the carriage back   and forth
across needles that clicked
like tongues recounting tales

and songs in shades   hues   subtle tones
weaving a myriad of dreams
whispered fables   in a web of colour

6.

Anne in a summer dress
slight willowy
evening light fired the grass
her eyes said *follow me*

mosses ferns lining the lane
beneath the hawthorns shadowy
a yearning I could never explain
her eyes said *follow me*

where ragged robin tufted vetch water mint
lady's smock
willow alder meadow sweet lady's bedstraw
haze and heat
light and shade speckled ground the air is filled
with thistle down

now all that remains
are the rags and tags of memory
a meadow a lane a dream
of eyes that said *follow me*

7.

she shredded & rewrote the holy word
with raven songs & spectral tales

she was spindrift in the moonlight gale
froth & spume in the gown of night

she spun & unspun yarns of light
she sang & painted sacred whispers

in shadowed halls where spirits linger
with vanishings & visions blurred

8.

a silhouette in the doorway
a drop of the hard stuff   just a drop
the long road to God alone knows where
L Cohen's *famous blue raincoat*
a bottle of pills spilt over the tabletop
a handwritten note
a moment alone   just a moment
a desperate embrace   a kiss   a cry

all you need to say goodbye

9.

beyond millennia
  flood & flow
storm   tide   wash

eight thousand years
  & more   yet
footprints remain

in the estuarine sludge

  a wet brilliance
  the sweep of the ebb
the airy distance

  children
    adults
      herons
        fishers all

 willow withies woven
   with skill
    cunning
& a wise woman's charms

only imagine   a resonance

in the air
      the sea breeze
   their laughter
 their song

Linda Moore

Every flower blooms

In its own time

Originally from Omagh, Linda Moore, now a retired school teacher, lives in the village of Ballykelly on the banks of the River Foyle in Northern Ireland.

While she was studying, her writing was on factual findings, whereas at home writing consists of shopping and to do lists.

After joining a Creative writing group Linda is enjoying the learning process and taking on board this new challenge.

Red Pen Phobia

as a young girl I loved to write about

the excitement of flying a kite

rustling leaves as we ran through them

the sounds of the sea   the feel of the waves

what we did at the weekend

my stories were long with lots of 'and then'

in my happy place free and light

always ten out of ten

one day I wrote "*what s'wrong* "

not knowing the S belonged to the *what*

there on my page the dreaded red

no explanation   no correction   no suggestion

no longer ten out of ten

my happy place turned to fear of that red

I wrote as little as I could

but still the red was there

in English class I switched off

no good at this

why should I care.

sixty years later I joined a writing group

why? I'll never know

the fear still there   I didn't feel right

I'll sit   watch   pretend I am shy

but wait ! no red in sight

I may never have work in print

perhaps that'd be pie in the sky

but thank you for letting me write

for giving me a safe place to try

We will remember them

Standing alone in the house which once was his family home, Joe undid the strings around the letters he had sent home. His family had moved to a smaller house closer to his Dad's work during the war. Able to regain his status as gardener on the estate - wanting to be alone, away from people and noise - he was relieved to find his old home was still available to rent.

A bed sat alone in the bedroom while in the kitchen stood a dresser and a stove which still worked. Behind the door stood the table Joe had reclaimed from the woodshed, with a repaired chair tucked under it. On the table sat an oil lamp, his only means of light during the dark hours. The well in the garden provided fresh spring water. He had everything he needed.

Looking at his scribbled notes sent from the trenches reminded Joe of having to share pencils or pens to write his letters in semi-darkness, rushing to catch the post. Thinking about the trenches - the smell of urine, the smoke in the distance, the lukewarm food, the fear in everyone's eyes - he knew those memories would stay with him forever.

When it rained a battlefield was a damp place to be, with the water running off the fields into the trenches. Sometimes it was like a river finding its way to the sea, often mixed with the blood of the wounded. Lying covered with a heavy blanket on cold wet ground with little time for sleep, the men were tired, afraid, longing for home.

All the troops looked forward to receiving letters from home though it was difficult to know what to write back. Not being allowed to reveal any war information left nothing else to say. Asking about family and friends, about what they were doing or thanking people for their letters and gifts became the main content of their replies.

Smiling at his letters he realised that in them he was always asking for tobacco for his pipe. Looking at his pipe now half-lit, Joe thought how it had been a comfort to him, with or without tobacco. Receiving hand knit socks had always been a welcome gift for frozen feet. Squished cakes, although no longer edible, had reminded him of the family sitting round the kitchen table. Longing for these presents or letters telling him about the news from home had kept him going during the terrible fearful days

Joe turned to the letter dated 19th June 1917, the one telling the family how his brother John had found him before he'd left for the battlefield. They had been so pleased to see each other, although he'd added that John had suffered an injury "*a bullet in the head*." His eyes misted over as he recalled his next letter from home which had informed him that after that meeting John had died on

15th June. He had been too young to die, only four months before his twenty first birthday, four years younger than him.

Joe folded the letters, tied them up again with the string before wrapping his medals in a torn flour bag. Placing them both at the back of the dresser drawer, he felt he did not deserve them. All he had done was to keep his head down. How he wished John had done the same.

He closed the drawer on that part of his life.

Dancing the night away

~ extract from my memoir ~

The Sailor's Hornpipe. That was start of my love for dancing. The *Scottish Sword Dance* followed. Partnered with my uncle on bagpipes, entertaining the family as they clapped along, I danced on my grandmother's worn rug in the dim room lit by a gas mantle overhead. Dancing around with my arms in the air, my skirt swinging to the beat, I was in my happy place.

I loved to dance.

Going out to dance was known as going to a Social. My first was at our local Scout Hall. As a ten-year-old, I was so excited to be allowed to attend. The only downside was you had to walk in with a Scout. Desmond was in my class at school. I liked him, but he asked May to go with him. I had to make do with his friend Rodger who had a runny nose, and was not as tall as me. But what mattered was I was getting to a social!

After paying our 1s/6d entry fee, we left our coats in a cloakroom (a thing in those days), then entered the main hall which was decorated in bunting to make it look more inviting. The Scout Master sat with his record player on one table while on the other was a pile of singles and LP's which belonged to individual Scouts. No-one minded the records were scratched. Sometimes the needle jumped tracks. But it was music. We were dancing.

I loved to dance.

At fourteen I was old enough to attend a Social in other halls where live bands provided the music. Before stepping out to these events it was necessary to visit the make-up counter at Woolworths where one of everything was compulsory. Wearing my Sunday clothes with badly put on make-up including clear nail varnish not only on my nails but also on my stockings to prevent runs, I felt very glamorous. Along with my friends we would rush in as soon as the doors opened. It was more expensive, costing 2s to enter. The cloakroom was free, but you had to make sure not to lose your ticket or you'd have to stay behind until all the other coats were claimed.

At the venue for our first teenage social we climbed the worn stairs, entering the main hall, dark, musty, heavily curtained. Old-fashioned faded portraits framed the walls overlooking the chairs which lined three sides of it. On the remaining side was the stage where the live band would perform. We always sat near it, opposite the main entrance to get an unobstructed view of who was arriving.

Music was played in sets of three songs. One set would be fast songs where we would be first up bopping in front of the stage. The alternate sets were slow songs requiring a male to dance. For those we sat watching, praying for a boy to ask us to dance. While the dance band had their break halfway through, we made our way downstairs where we were given a bun, washed down with a cup of tea. As the evening progressed with everyone moving to the music, the mixture of mustiness, sweat, and the over-perfumed dancers was pungent. Fresh air was welcome when we left the building after the National Anthem.

Dance halls differed in their rules. Several places provided a drink in a glass bottle with a straw accompanied by a bag of crisps. Not all halls played the same National Anthem; it was wise to pay attention to where you were. Boys sat on one side of the hall with girls on the other. At the end of each dance set the church leaders walked up the middle of the hall separating the couples. Not that it bothered me. I was not interested in boys except as a dance partner where necessary.

I loved to dance

As older teenagers we stopped going to socials, but now danced in ballrooms. We began to follow *Showbands*. Travelling with our favourite band, which we knew from school, worked well for us. Free travel, free entry to the event, a supper afterwards but the most exciting part was dancing all night to our favourite musicians. Travelling great distances to dance to our favourite bands, we were in a dancehall when the first shots of the Troubles were fired nearby. We were locked in. The upside of this was that the band played an extra half hour.

I acquired my first car, a Mini. There was no stopping us now. We followed various bands, soon learning to always have means of identification when stopped at roadblocks. Also, it was wise to have a plan B just in case there was a bomb scare at our chosen venue.

I loved to dance

Then it all went terribly wrong. The trend changed. No longer were crowds going to large ballrooms. Instead, young people were meeting in bars which had no dance area. Now dances were held in lounges with music provided by one man carrying a posh record player with a bundle of records. These were called discothèques, later known as Discos as no-one could spell the word. This was evident from the handwritten posters on the doors which replaced the colourful ones which had once adorned the entrances to ballrooms.

Everyone was talking, laughing, ignoring the music. The DJ, as the record changer was known, could have played the same record all night. I don't think anyone would have noticed. With the strange lighting everyone looked like they were wearing their underwear on the outside. As for dancing, there was an allotted space which might have held six people. I was only twenty-five. My social life was over.

Would I ever dance again?

~ to be continued ~

Janet Peace

'The secret of life is enjoying the passage of time', James Taylor

Janet Peace is a retired educationalist living near the spectacular North Coast of Northern Ireland. Since joining North Coast Writers, she has enjoyed the experience of sharing in the diverse creativity of the group and been encouraged and inspired by all its members. Writing jostles for position with pottering about in the garden and caring for a household of rescue cats and an old border-collie. Her large family, many pets, stunning location and reflections on life all inspire her poetry.

In 2022 her poems appeared in the anthology *Love, Loss and Cardiac Issues* and in *Springboards: A Manual of Creative Writing,* both published by Impspired Press. In 2023 her poem *'The Last Dance'* featured in both the Impspired Online Magazine No 21 and print edition Volume 11. Her work also featured in two more North Coast Writers Anthologies, *Spun Tales and Woven words 2023, and Seaspray and Woodland Glades, 2024,* as well as in *Writing from the Heart*, collated by Jae Jenkins Smith and Rob Taylor, 2025 all published by Impspired Press.

Author of the Dedication poem
at the beginning of this Anthology

The train ride between Derry Londonderry and Coleraine has been described by Michael Palin as "One of the most beautiful rail journeys in the World".

The railway track runs alongside the golden sands of Benone Strand on the North Coast of Ireland before tunnelling beneath maritime cliffs at Downhill.

Coast Train

Looking out through strumming glass
Foyles estuary banks begin to beach
lllllllllllllllllllllllllllllllllllllllllllllllllllllllI
a hack of horses gather p a c e and
r a c e and c h a s e giant metal beast

Benone has m i l e s of golden sand
which st r e t ch beside the railway track
llllllllllllllllllllllllllllllllllllllllllllllllllllllll
beachcombers sift bare-footers dip
sea-mermaids chat in coffee shack

sand-artists rake kites rise and dive
linked couples talk & smile & stroll
lllllllllllllllllllllllllllllllllllllllllllllllllllllllI
striped beachballs r o l l score a goal
blue flags stiff-breeze lifeguards patrol

dog-walkers p a u s e a frisbee soars
keen jogs delay while families play
lllllllllllllllllllllllllllllllllllllllllllllllllllllllI
surfboarders crest wild spuming waves
sunbathers l a z e the day away

B&B by the sea favoured by celebrity
Downhills before train tunnels right neath
lllIIIIIIIIIIIIIIIIIIIIIIIIIIIIIIIIIIIIIIIIII
Mussenden iconic sight small temple
edge - perched .... on cliffs height

At Castlerock rough sand dunes flank
fine golf-links course to rivers bank
llllllllllllllllllllllllllllllllllllllllllllllllllIIIII
players braced by briny air stroll holes
club-house .... drink pinot- blanc

by tidal rib sanderlings s k i p
keen anglers bait from Barmouth end
llllllllllllllllllllllllllllllllllllllllllllllllllIIII
Yawl sails on jib small row boats skiff
sky mellows as mist-haze descends

Bann f l o w s to sea at estuary
fowl w a d e fresh sea-salts brackish flow
llllllllllllllllllllllllllllllllllllllllllllllllllIIII
coaches s l o w down on entering town
folk disembark .... faces aglow

D for Daughter

At the back of your old-man drawer

three handkerchiefs found

finest Irish linen

washed-thin   folded   ironed-flat

into chocolate-bar squares

scented faintly with cedar and musk

corners initialled in blue

D for Douglas

D for dad

D for deceased

Nanny's Last Hoot

blue lights outside
cooled the glow of fairy lights
slow-fading through the window

an old dog raised his head
stretched   sighed   snoozed on
as the pendulum of a gingerbread clock
wonkily   ticked   down   time

in the hearth
cremating yule-logs
sparked amid amber embers
haloed by hypnotic flames
writhing in a ghostly dance

she sat propped by cushions

and cats   snuggled up close

her knitting had slipped some stitches

a book had lost its page

her phone lay on her lap

hello caller   is the patient breathing

an ambulance is on its way

a disembodied voice announced

ice melted in a glass of Baileys

as Jules hoot-nannied in another New Year

Jazz and Blues

He perches on a drunken stool

wearing cool black Stetson

shab-leather coat

shredding riffs from battered Gibson

phrasing octaves freed to

f o t

l a

lit cigarette butt

burns under catgut

smoke-signals curls

Purple Haze

glows red to the beat

builds up white-heat

veils his blood-veined gaze

synchronized drinks

vibrate and clink

line 'em up

line 'em up on the stage

insensate swigs

at soulless gigs

assuage artistic rage

with heavy gait

blank   gaping stare

he stumbles in

slumps on the bed

the stale odorous reek

of his vodka-soaked breath

clings to linen

hangs foul in the air

Red Bull

it's not the dawn chorus gentling me from sleep

but a deep   hollow   bellow

from the solitary bull

grazing wildflower meadow

magnificent beast   excluded from the herd

mourning his exile   hollering despair

a bovine king without his kine

his offspring   sired for slaughter

and what of the young beeves   nibbling the hedge

who jostle for position

push   shove   to hear the sizzle

as we barbecue the steaks

the ribeye and the rump

spitting juices on the coal

do they know that as they gaze

they're bred for slaughter

Hazel Siberry

Like a bird on a Wire
I have tried in my way
to be free

A retired GP, Hazel Siberry lives in the beautiful seaside village of Castlerock on the Causeway Coast in Northern Ireland. After retirement she joined a Creative Writing Group just for fun and is enjoying it as a challenge. She has had five of her pieces published in *Woodland Glades and Sea Spray*, an Anthology of Writing from the North Coast of Ireland, published by Impspired, 2024.

Fox

one summertime night

in dawns amber glow

split by a screaming

vixen   roadkill   show

red brush in red pool

two cubs seem to know

fox instinct no fool

to this vulpine keening

I imbue human feeling

when their parents die

do all fox cubs cry

of course they do

Reunion

fifty-five years past   sensing vocation
naïve young students   alive with ambition
one hundred fresh faces   ideals ablaze
Civil Rights marches   Belfast's dark days
no dance halls or concerts   our social life dead
Guinness free for Blood Donors instead

twenty years flown   by then we were scattered
burnt out by The Troubles   ideals shattered
some to the Missions   others   scarred   moved away
to more peaceful countries   with much better pay
busy building   lives   family   home and career
no urge to return for Reunion "that" year

fifty years since degree   most feel that it matters
high flying specialists   GPs   Deans   Professors
looking so prosperous   same faces   just older
discussing lost friends   thoughts become sober
fun   laughter   mad antics   wild days of our past
these   we remember   not bullet or blast

another Reunion
but is
"this"
the last?

Our Day Out 1959

family outing   summer morning
excited all   at Crumlin boarding
old steam train   ten coaches lurching
huffing   chuffing   white smoke puffing
windows down   bodies dangling
eager   soot-smeared   faces laughing
rattling on to Causeway Coast

armed with buckets   castles building
cold sea water   causing shrieking
knitted costume   wet wool sagging
furtively   in bath towels changing
cones or sliders   ice cream dripping
sandy sandwich   egg and onion
warm C&C's   brown lemonade

cardigan clad   becoming nippy
frantic race to local chippy
instead of fries with garlic dips
newspaper covered fish and chips
soused with salt   malt vinegar steaming
tired feet
          but faces beaming
                              reluctantly
                                        to train
                                              and
                                                    home

Slough of Despond

Mary was always immaculate. Even walking her dog Alfie, she always wore full make up and a dressy outfit to boost self-esteem. Severe back pain had caused a change in her routine: she now walked Alfie through the Castle grounds daily, the exercise beneficial for her mobility and mental wellbeing. Alfie, after monthly salon visits, always looked smart.

Two days of torrential rain had curtailed their walks. A sunny Sunday morning, even with a chilly wind, encouraged both to resume their exercise. Mary set off in a new faux fur coat, purchased online at considerable expense. Alfie, having just been to the salon, looked like a white puff ball.

Repair work was being carried out on certain paths. On Sundays no workmen were present. One of the paths was dug up, now covered by black plastic, muddy with rain and pedestrian traffic.

Alfie spotted a grey squirrel and bolted towards it. The lead reached its limit, the jerk causing Mary to slip, tumbling face first into a deep muddy ditch. Attempts to lever herself up using her walking pole were impossible, the pole disappearing into sludge. The more she tried to get purchase with her walking boots, the farther they sank. The mud like wet quicksand, her boots were soon full.

Beginning to panic, Mary spotted some tourists ambling towards the Castle. Putting her arm in the air like a drowning woman, she shouted "HELP". The group looked towards her. Seeing only a raised arm, they smiled and gave her a friendly wave before continuing their walk. Alfie, thinking this a great game, jumped in. Soon he was also stuck.

Bloody tourists! Useless! Now you too! She groaned.

She felt herself sink deeper. Frightened, she remembered her phone in an inside pocket. Inserting her hand to retrieve it, the inside of her faux fur coat was soon full of mud. Opening the phone, she managed to speed-dial Jane, praying that she would answer.

Jane, busy in her garden, took the call.

HELP ME   Please

At first, Jane thought it a practical joke, but hearing panic in Mary's voice she agreed to come to the rescue. The Entry Gate to the Castle Grounds was locked. Abandoning her Jeep, carrying two large umbrellas with curved handles, she raced towards the ditch. There she found Mary and Alfie, both a mud-mired mess.

Grasping both umbrella handles, Mary was pulled out with a loud glooping sound. Once secure, Jane used a single handle to hook Alfie's harness, extracting him from the quagmire. Like creatures arisen from a swamp, they squelched to the Jeep, their muddy state causing astonished glances from other walkers. Jane felt laughter bubble up inside her; it had to be supressed. Mary was not in the mood for humour.

At the Jeep, the next problem arose. A plastic passenger seat cover and mat gave some protection. For Alfie, the back was lined with Shopping Bags for Life.

Back home, Jane entered, opening the back door. Outside stood Mary and Alfie, mud starting to dry on them both. Desperate measures were called for; a handy garden hose was employed to remove the worst of the glaur.

Provided with a dressing gown, Mary stripped off; even her underwear was mud soaked. As she headed for a shower, Jane piled all her clothes, boots, dog harness and lead, even her faux fur coat, with its DRY CLEAN ONLY label, into the washing machine.

Now it was Alfie's turn. Filling the sink with lukewarm water, elbow-tested to make sure it was not too hot, Alfie was immersed. Unaccustomed to such rough treatment, he struggled. Soon the kitchen was awash with soapy water; Jane was soaked. Laughter bubbling up, she was no longer able to control it. In a paroxysm, with tears streaming down her face, she had to sit down.

Towel turbaned, Mary returned to find Jane helpless with laughter. Alfie, restored to his normal white colour, stood forlorn, dripping wet in the middle of a swamped kitchen. At last, Mary saw the funny side. It took some time to recover their composure. Jane commented that she had often called Mary a stick-in-the-mud when she resisted change.

It took Jane two weeks to remove all traces of mud from her Jeep. Through the miracle of Vanish and Ariel Automatic, Mary's clothes were returned to their pristine state, even her walking boots and faux fur coat …

… but from then on Mary's nickname was "Old-Stuck-In-The-Mud".

This writing thing

'this writing thing...' is an informal voluntary networking group, for writers and emerging writers who meet once a month, based in Derry ~ Londonderry

Stan McWilliams *~ collator ~*

Let me live, love, and say it well in good sentences.

- The Unabridged Journals of Sylvia Plath, Sylvia Plath

A Donegal-based writer, Stan is the parent of three grown children, an organic farmer and wind farmer. His writing takes inspiration from a rural environment, and his Antrim and Leitrim roots.

After a career, encompassing engineering, teaching and farming, he started creative writing in 2019, producing a series of short stories as well as a mixture of memoirs, family-related tales and fiction. With work published in the Leitrim Guardian, Fingerpost, The Corran Herald, The Bangor Literary Review, The Galway Review, and in the Ulster-Scots publication Yarns, he has also contributed to the Bloody Sunday 50th Anniversary Community Writing Archive and read his work at Tenx9 and Culture Night events. A winner of the annual Impspired Soundwaves Competition in 2024 for the prose piece *Let's Meet at Carnlough*, he has been awarded bursaries to the John Hewitt Summer School and the Tyrone Guthrie Centre, both in Ireland.

While drafts of the stories can be seen in his regular blog www.thecurlewscall.com, he is a member of the Derry writing group "this writing thing", the Irish Writer's Union and the Irish Writer's Centre.

Close shave

Then he came to shave my chest. And with him, a chill wind that blew away any remaining nonchalance. Practiced and casual, he talked in soothing Dublin tones; yet held something back, expectant, prepared perhaps for an unwanted confession.

Not much view from this ward, is there? he asserted as the buzzing trimmer stroked my skin, his breath mint-fresh. We both knew the plans for the next few hours started with heavy sedation. The view would be irrelevant. But would the scalpel make one clean incision? How could I not feel it?

Still, you're better in here on a day like that. Would the battery of the sternal saw be fully charged? Vibrate? Spit out fragments of my bone?

You're from somewhere north of the Liffey? he joked, brushing the trimmer's teeth clean, grey hairs falling, collecting on my sheeted lap. Always greyer when cut and gathered. How many green scrubs and masked faces would gather around me? All at their day's work. Tired perhaps?

I spent a summer in Donegal years ago. What a time. How do you stop and start a heart? Slice it open to reveal the damaged flap of my mitral valve? Will the surgeon hold my heart in his hand?

Is it a wonder that I floated back into a disturbing brown dystopia – prompted, I was later told, by my sci-fi readings - where comfortless and ghostly shapes watched and minded my vitals, as others lay, similarly wired and tubed, in beds held sloped in the octagonal intensive care room: of a doomed space ship stranded light years from home?

From the faint dim walls around me, diamond patterns grew into the form of dark heads and faces. They waited motionless, their distant gaze unconcerned it seemed. Waiting for what? Some atonement or recompense? From me? Then left in their own silent time as they had come, morphing back into shadow. Others were to follow with disturbing regularity. Nothing was familiar. Nothing brought comfort.

A few days later these delusions faded into the normalcy of the hospital ward. And now, months later, I can now recount all this with a smile, a steady breath and a strong heartbeat.

On Europe's Salty Rim

they play on a shore
far from death's hungry grasp
a sheltered North Atlantic summer
the air balmy on the tide of change

Amira and brother Ahmed
and Juno
Juno a name that fell on him for a new life
unknown among the survivors

they splash and yelp as one
spin a swim ring of smiling fish
to be caught on outstretched arms
that jump from the shallows

a cheer for the catch
a groan for the lost
they thrash and cry
on Europe's salty rim

innocence plays on a shore
far from death's hungry grasp

Running the Phoenix Park 2022
~ for Berenice

all autumn sunshine and chill
the Phoenix Park is crisp
two of us on a Sunday morning run
religiously
fit and fluid for our years
breathing in the moment
our worn soles lightening
around and between the
brunched green revellers
families holding back children and dogs
grasses bent under strolling figures long gone

a sudden gust cuts across the parkland
ducking under trees
drawing a wheezy breath
storms through an ancient beech
it carries
a swirling leafy eddy
flashed iridescent by the low sun
then gone
spent
a shower of twisting gold
fluttering to the ground

our stride in tune
keeps pace
breathing long settled
snaking a path back to the car

You Have My Ear

I was brought up very strict. Presbyterian strict. Daily church activities become part of the amalgam of who you are. You're unaware of any other way of being. Or seeing. But teenage years bring change. It can go any way.

I was going to church two to three times on Sundays then. At the Boys Brigade and church youth club, maybe four times a week. Enjoying most of it: camping out on the Antrim Hills in summer, winter evenings of boys letting loose, tidying up a pensioner's garden, weekend trips away or Saturday evenings raucous in a Portrush swimming pool, the camaraderie and the crack.

On Sundays wearing a suit I never liked, never wearing it out. I couldn't say all of this was against my will. I was the fourth generation steeped in our church and its traditions. Hellfire preachers were brought in once or twice a year to get our souls over the blessed line. These were uncomfortable occasions, feeling the heat of God's stare on you. There in your pew. Anxious at being told this may be your *very last* offer of salvation. Feelings of relief and guilt as the decision was fudged again.

By mid-teens, my world of Ballymena and our church began to feel claustrophobic. I sensed a bigger place elsewhere. Sensed change.

A couple of years later, with a group of friends, I started to skip Sunday morning service. We would be at the tail end of the crowd going into the church – the meeting house us plain-speaking Presbyterians called them – but we'd turn sharply and walk off up the empty street. We had about an hour and a half to ourselves and headed for the People's Park, walking its many paths and generally messing about. One or two always offered stories of recent exploits with girlfriends, different from those they'd told a few weeks before. On our return to the church we would seamlessly join the worshippers leaving, going home to their Sunday lunch. Morning service was always full. No one ever noticed a half dozen missing souls. Not Daddy, anyway. And the subject of the sermon never came up at Sunday lunch. Though I strongly suspect that six young fellas in suits strolling the quiet Sunday morning streets were a giveaway.

But before those Sundays came music. And girls. Music started it, with Procol Harum's Whiter Shade of Pale. I was fifteen, hormones starting to surge. The song was the number-one hit all summer long. Playing on the radio. In shops and cafes. It drifted through open doors onto the sunny streets. Played over the Tannoy on agricultural show day, over the preened cattle and shiny new-model tractors. The sound of the churchy Hammond organ and the cryptic lyrics wrapped me in pleasure and hope. Later, they called it *The Summer of Love*. It was one of those innocent summers before all hell broke loose.

I had no idea what the song's lyrics meant. It didn't matter. The song painted my imagination in colours that wouldn't fade. The images were brighter and fresher than the repetition of Bible stories which reduced them to doom-laden prophecies. Perhaps the organ's breathy notes made it instantly familiar: a cross-over hymn. The song's images were gossamer yet clear, evocative yet ambiguous, heavenly yet earthy. The organ lifted. The familiar chorus. I'm gone.

And so it was that later
As the miller told his tale
That her face, at first just ghostly
Turned a whiter shade of pale

If the song opened a window to an alluring world, it also started a struggle within me that would see-saw on for years. For a while, in late teens, this seemed relentless. The internal squabbling would eventually quieten, though it would take years to stop finally. In our faith, it's a personal crusade. It's my battle with the Devil in all his forms. An internal battle for the most part. You win out and proclaim that you are 'saved by the blood of Jesus', or you don't and remain beguiled by Satan, lost to an eternity of Hell's fires. There's no middle way there. It's stark, God or the Devil. The first line of our BB anthem went 'Onward Christian soldiers, marching as to war.' Despite all, I was beginning to turn my back on that march and move in another direction.

There was a multitude of other songs I remember that year: The Monkees' *I'm a Believer,* The Beatles' *Strawberry Fields,* The Stones' *Ruby Tuesday,* Scott McKenzie's *San Francisco,* Pink Floyd's *See Emily Play,* Jackie Wilson's *Your Love*, Jimmy Hendrix's *Hey Joe,* and that's not half of them. They all helped colour my world, and clear my grey Ulster skies. They all had my ear. But for me, *A Whiter Shade of Pale* marked a beginning.

Florence Forbes

Florence Forbes, born in Northern Ireland, writes mostly poetry, but occasionally strays into short stories. She regularly attends workshops and is a member of two Creative Writing groups, *Foyle u3a Writers Group* and *this writing thing*.

Performing poetry at Pushkin Trust events, she has also read at various local Open Mic events. On four occasions in 2022 and 2023, she performed her prose pieces at Tenx9.

Her pieces have been published in various anthologies. *Garden Poem* was published in *Voices of 100 Women Anthology* in 2011. The prose piece *Paradise will be a kind of Library* and the poem *Bury Me in the Library* were both in the Collection *Bury Me in the Library*, published by *Guildhall Press*, 2017. Two CAP Anthologies featured her Poems -*Together* in *Vision, 2020* and *Just a slip of the tongue* in *Manifest*, 2024. *The Arts Council of NI* published her poem *The Seahorse Path* in the Collection *More Questions about Butterflies*, also in 2024. Between 2019 and 2024, Florence had fourteen Limericks published in The Daily Mail newspaper.

Ukraine

I read the papers, listen to the radio and watch the television. It is so distressing. Hard to believe that it has seemingly happened so suddenly. The need to go somewhere for a while to avoid hearing more devastating news overwhelms me. In the past, my garden has always given me somewhere to relax and be happy.

There are some bulbs which I had been meaning to plant. I read the instructions.

First, prepare the ground. Dig a deep hole, three times the size of the bulbs.

I put my foot on the spade and push. It doesn't penetrate the ground as far as it should. That's when I discover that some nearby trees or shrubs have sent out multiple rhizomes. I find the secateurs and attack the straggling roots. I had never come across such thuggish behaviour before. They gave the appearance of wanting to take over the whole garden. How dare they! Their selfish behaviour would ultimately lead to the destruction of the smaller plants. After a lot of hard work, the area is cleared. Before carrying on, I sit on an old stump of a dead tree to get back my breath. My eyes wander to the edges of the garden. The slight breeze makes the blue and yellow irises blur into a flag. Concentrate. Read the next instruction.

Plant the bulbs - at least an inch apar, with the narrow part at the top, and cover with the soil.

I fetch the well-worn kneeling pad and space the bulbs out as suggested. They are supposed to be placed in a random fashion so that they will grow in more natural looking clumps. In their rigid lines, they remind me of a picture I saw once after the excavation of the Terracotta Warriors in China. What is it about all-powerful leaders that they so fear death? Dear God, do they really think that statues of soldiers are going to prevent them from being dragged into the burning fires of hell?

I cover the bulbs with a mixture of soil and compost. Still on my knees, I read the final instruction.

Water well.

No need to reach for the watering can. The tears are flowing steadily down my cheeks.

Unstoppable.

A Day After

The beach was full of sunbathers. Children were building sandcastles. Sometimes a younger child would swat one of the turrets with his spade to the dismay of an older sibling. Some settled for the rhythmic sound of the tide coming in as it hit the nearby rocks.

On the wall behind the sand, people sat with their backs to the sea, chatting to friends. There was a special hum from conversations in various languages, mostly European. Others strolled along the walkway with their dogs. Such a variety would rarely be seen in the rural areas at home. It was obvious that these well-groomed animals were regarded as much-loved members of the families who frequently had to open up a plastic bag and scoop up the doggy deposits.

A man sat on a portable stool playing his guitar effortlessly whilst the barefooted girl in her swirling skirt danced with a hoop hypnotising anyone who stopped to watch.

The sun suddenly seemed to dive behind the only cloud in the sky. Nearly everyone looked up anxiously, fearing that their relaxing day could be cut short but relief showed on their faces as they realised that the cloud had no companions that day.

Along the beach the green flag blew gently beside the viewpoint where the lifeguard constantly scanned the water. No excitement today. The day before had provided enough of that. But people forget easily. The sun and sea drew them back constantly.

Perchance to Dream

Last night I went to bed, perchance to dream
of writing rhythmic words for next week
But first of all I have to chance upon a theme.

And when I choose a subject, not too bleak
I'll tenderly display my chosen lines
in format designed by an ancient Greek.

I'm told that verses have a need of rhymes
in the writing of a Terza Rima
while repeating words cause echoing chimes.

As I thought, what word would rhyme with Rima
I drifted off to sleep and so to dream
of exotic festivals in Lima.

Where I rumbaed in dresses quite extreme
before I went to bed, perchance to dream

Fight the Good Fight

“Drop the fight tomorrow. You’ll get more than enough to cover your debts,” said Michael, my manager.

"What was I going to do?"

I looked in the mirror. Unusually for a boxer, my nose remained unbroken. The face reflected back at me looked the same as it had every other day of my life. Today was different. Able to look at the rest of my body and admire the muscles bulging from my arms and chest, see the skin glistening from the rubbed-in oil, I couldn’t look into my own eyes.

Why had I ever let myself be put into such a position? It’s not as if I hadn’t been warned. My father’s voice rang in my head.

“Gambling is the work of the devil. Hard work is the only way to earn money.”

I had worked hard, earned money. Trouble was I'd given in to the temptation of the casino. When I listened to my father’s advice, I didn’t even know what a casino was. That came after I'd won my first championship. I was feted by so many of my heroes and introduced to places I had never dreamed of. Over the years, every time I won another match, more and more of my winnings were lost to the tables in the casino.

I hit rock bottom.

How I longed to be back in Ireland. To be able to sit down with my father, talk through my troubles with him. Would he understand? Would he forgive me for bringing shame on to the family if it came out what I was considering?

Looking in the mirror again, tears blurred the image. I found myself looking at my father instead of myself. For years I'd looked up to him as well as up at him in the pulpit. Sitting between my sister and mother, I'd absorbed the weekly lesson. The mixture of "dos and do nots" but also the words of love and forgiveness.

Don't kid yourself, I told myself. Dad would never agree with what I was considering. What use would it be talking it over with him? I knew what he'd say. This was a decision I would have to make myself.

My dressing room door opened. Michael walked in . "Two minutes to go. Well, are you going to do it?" The eyes in the mirror closed as I took a deep breath.

Walking into the ring I heard the usual cheers, as the referee lifted my arm, walked me round the ring shouting his usual words of how great I was. It sounded like waves crashing over the rocks in the west of Donegal. Faces blurred until I caught sight of one man in the front row. I stared at him. My father. He was here. Alone.

He'd always said neither he nor my mother would ever come to any of my fights, watching someone hitting me. It didn't mean that he wasn't proud of me.

He just couldn't watch. Now he was here, on this night of all nights. I didn't have time to say anything but I could feel something inside me change.

The bell rang. The fight began. I forgot everything, lost myself in the moment. Only when the referee held up my arm again announcing that I'd won did I realise what I had done. I looked over to where my father had been sitting but he was no longer there. Back in the dressing room, Michael was jumping up and down with rage.

"Have you any idea of the mess you've left me in. What the hell are you playing at."

"I haven't time for this now. I need to find my father."

"Your father never comes to see you. What makes you think he's here now?"

I rang home to ask my mother what had changed his mind.

Her voice sounded so strange.

"I didn't want to tell you just before your fight. Your father had a heart attack and died. I want you home."

Getting a taste for it

I waited for him to die. Savoured the familiar excitement. Not quite as good as the first time but still leaving me feeling a high. The first time hadn't been planned at all. Maybe that's why it was different.

Learning The Knowledge to become a taxi driver in London had taken longer than I'd imagined. I'd been working for another two years before I picked up this particular fare. My cab was parked in a rank near Buckingham Palace. I was listening *to Son of a Preacher Man,* a new release by Dusty Springfield. Not quite sure whether I liked her or not.

A dark night, he didn't recognise me but then I am sure that I looked somewhat different. He hadn't changed one bit since we'd last met; older for sure but still that same sadistic smirk. Still such a 'here's me and there's nobody like me' type of man. He didn't deign to have a conversation with a lowly cabbie. He was so absorbed in his paperwork that he didn't even notice when I took a detour. He did look surprised when I parked the taxi in an old disused garage I owned.

"What the ...," he muttered looking up from the folder in his lap. "What the hell are we doing here?"

He tried to open his door which I had locked. His mouth fell open when he realized that I was attaching a rubber tube from the exhaust into the taxi. He had still not recognised me, so I placed my face close to the window until at last, his pupils dilated black with a belated sign of recognition.

As I watched him screaming, hammering on the windows, I smiled. I never thought I'd get the chance to torture him the way he tortured me in school. Then he'd taken every opportunity to use the cane he kept hooked on the back of his chair. A jury made up from the rest of my class would never have convicted me.

His body relaxed as if he had fallen asleep except for the sweaty handprint on the glass. He had finally succumbed to the poisonous gases. I opened the front windows and drove the taxi to nearby Epping Forest where I dumped his body with neither respect nor ceremony. As I drove off, I left the windows down until no smell of the gases could be detected.

Stopping at a late-night corner shop I bought a few tins of air freshener.

"Bloody drunks," I said to the cashier who nodded sympathetically. "Sick all over my taxi. Then I can't take any more fares. I want to swing for some of them."

"Yeah, I know," he agreed. "I get a lot of them, causing trouble when they've had a few. Mind you, it's the parents I blame."

Paying for the sprays, I left. Radioing in to the office with this version of events I headed home earlier than usual.

Months afterwards, when there was no longer any mention of the dead man on the news or in the newspapers, I remember feeling almost let down. I should have felt happy having disposed of someone who had spoiled so much of my childhood but the feeling didn't last.

Finding myself thinking of other people who had been nasty to me, I started to plan the killings. Of course, I dumped the bodies in different locations. Not always easy as I'm not strong but I learned to park the taxi on an incline. Then the body would roll out with not too much effort. Once in Richmond Park, I tied a rope from the body to an oak tree, driving off a little until it was dragged clear of the taxi. That was the first time that I thought I was going to be caught. Turned out to be some of the deer having a late night snack of the acorns lying nearby. I didn't do any more for quite a long time after that.

How I loved to listen to the police appealing for anyone with any information. I used to laugh at that. Those years working hard to acquire The Knowledge to be a taxi driver. Now I was working just as hard to improve my knowledge of killing.

After disposing of all those who had annoyed me in the past, with a taste for it now, I started to pick random customers. I needed the high.

This last one started to annoy me as soon as he got into my taxi.

"Westminster. Make it snappy. I'm in a hurry."

I turned to look at him as he spread himself out, folding his overcoat before carefully placing it on the seat beside him.

Fastidious. They were the worst.

"Time you had a manicure. Your nail polish is badly chipped."

Brian Hasson

Born in Derry, Northern Ireland, Brian is a care assistant for Adults with Learning Disabilities in Daycare. The author of *A Collection of Short Stories, Poems and Memoir,* self-published through Amazon in 2021, his love for writing and creativity stems from his admiration for the work of other local authors. He attends a local writing group *this writing thing* as often as he can as well as attending the many various Courses which run in his local area. Enjoying writing in a variety of genres - poetry and haiku in particular - he never travels anywhere without his pocket notebook or pen.

Seaview

Grass hedges wildly overgrown,

flakes of paint descend from the gate

the walls décor drape in a rustic theme

once a sight for sore eyes   now an eyesore

Forgotten how busy the road could be

Cars   lorries   buses whizz by

patient I wait. A safe gap appears

one final check of each side before I cross

Across the road hasn't changed

golf course   crooked steps to the beach.

Lough Swilly waves roar rough   carrying

a dry sharp wind   triggering a tear drop

The day is cold but clear memories glow

I picture the wee house in its glory

Malin Head on the right Fanad on the left

the wee house in Fahan right in the middle

Anger   sadness   outweighed with memories of old

grateful for those times   stories yet to be told

I don't know what made me stop today but clearly

hear Barney say *This is why I called it Seaview*.

Choices

(after Stopping by woods on a
Snowy Evening by Robert Frost)

Between the woods and frozen lake

neither path I wish to take

For survival I must choose one

I'll wait for the arrival of the sun

The sun rises, my path still not clear

no steps taken; I tremble with fear

The lake's surface covered with Ice and Snow

but the strength of it I do not know.

The trees in the woods whisper *Come, this way*

Beautiful to see but can I trust what they say?

I'll close my eyes; slowly breathe in

how did I get here, how did it begin?

Between the woods and frozen lake

which is the path I should take?

Will I open my eyes, let out a scream?

Maybe awaken, hoping it was a dream

Benone Strand

Carrying the weight of the world
he travels to the coast   alone
pressure of work   everyday life
his body's battery flat

A scenic route makes for an easy drive
Traffic light   just the right time of day
Einaudi plays   subtle in the background
as he looks forward to what's ahead

Destination reached he parks the car
there a young lady   needing
a short break too   she smiles
they embrace in a hug of friendship

With batteries repowering
they head for the beach
his heels heavy at first they sink but
upon harder sand flat footprints lie

Atlantic waves roar towards them
a bright joyful sun sharing its light
both pause   birds' chirp   horses trot
finding their space they decide to walk

Into the waves   up to their shins
chilling   refreshing Mussenden in sight
with sun heating their backs they casually chat
as time disappears they enjoy the stroll

Sitting on the beach they watch   they listen
to one another   to peace and tranquillity
they laugh they joke   just what was needed
time will reappear for work tomorrow

Mother n Nature

Crumbling sand concedes to my sinking heels
a tiny roar crashes   the tide is dwindling
silhouette hillside emerging without sunset backdrop
I'm no longer alone   eager strangers join too

The silence broken with an harmonious awe
at a night sky illuminated where Aurora now plays
mint green lights the base   medium purple above
Never seen its' like   Nature stuns!

My bright smile matches a woman nearby
her joyous reactions like a child on Christmas morn
A giggle escapes ... click! A perfect shot captured?
With my naked eye I see I've snatched the perfect shot

While I pour tea Aurora still plays and dances

Quickly she moves onto hide and seek   mostly hide

I'll cherish tonight's moments for as long as I live

time has no place here   Mother N Nature supreme

Nights of the Moon

I

Did you see the moon last night?

I did.

It made me gaze directly at it,

halved in size, precisely cut straight down the middle.

Right side in light, left side in dark.

A sandy glow outlines the dark clouds below the lighter ones.

First it was in front of me

-

next to my right,

then behind me -

finally taking refuge behind darkened clouds.

Did you see it?

II

Did you see the moon tonight?

I did!

More than a half-moon in size; oval shaped

Its sandy glow shows light clouds above, dark clouds below.

lighter tonight but still shining bright.

No matter which pane I look through, I see it.

Nature is breathtaking

with the power to make you stop   just watch,

drawn to its brightness even in the dark skies of night.

I wonder what the moon will show tomorrow?

Will you see it?

III

I watched for the moon tonight!

It's bigger, almost three quartered in size.

On its own tonight though, no clouds highlighted.

Tonight it sits lower, brighter too,

silhouetting rooftops of houses at the bottom of the square.

On its own, lonely yet powerful

in the still air of the night   nothing moves.

Three nights in a row I've watched the moon.

Did you see it?

IV

I was waiting for the moon tonight

It's grown is bigger though,

much brighter too, more whitish in colour.

Many stars accompany it tonight

Or was I so drawn by the beauty of previous moons,

I paid no attention to *them*?

Tonight even the stars shine bright.

I can't comprehend still that

even though they shine,

they have burnt out long ago.

Did you see the moon tonight?

V

Did you see the moon tonight?

I did!

It sits bold in the sky,

almost full moon.

It's glow vibrant, eye catching,

still shedding light

after the sun's dance today.

Stars are scattered.

No sounds heard as I make notes,

peaceful and calm.

Did you see the moon tonight?

VI

I have travelled most of today by bus and boat,

tired ready for bed I remember the moon.

High-rise buildings in Glasgow make it difficult to see

but I find a clear gap, there it sits   a full moon.

Complete in size, glittering bright.

Like a map, its craters highlighted.

Big city noises of busyness now

drowned by the moon's beauty.

Elated with what I see,

back in my accommodation

as I write my final notes,

I smile.

Did you see the moon this week?

I did.

Catherine Kay

~ drawn by Ciara Kay ~

There is a light that never goes out -
from lyrics by The Smiths

Catherine Kay lives in the wild and beautiful Inishowen Peninsula in Donegal, Ireland. Her writing has been performed in the Waterside Theatre, Derry, at The Words by the Water event, Greencastle and at Tenx9 events. She was long listed for the Cúirt New Writing Prize in 2023, and was highly commended in the Frances Browne Festival in 2023. Her poetry can be seen in the Storms Journal Anthology 4, 2024.

If I were CúChulainn

And so you called.
The raspy sadness in your voice
Caught me unawares

If I could
I'd rise Cú Chulainn-like
Leap the land's length
Flip-flopping; back-to-backing
Criss-crossing counties
Until I'd reached your grimy city door

There I would feed you pizza and hot chocolate
There I would hear each poignant essential woe
Forgiveness would sit between us
Shy and strong
Fat with generosity

In those concrete confines
Whilst Dublin sirens screeched
I would resist that urge to fold you in

my Bridget's cloak

To strap your defeated body on my back

To soar with you to the gold and purple hills of

Home

Listening for your words

I would begin again

Cut from you

the dull hessian binds of here

Offer instead

the silk-shot threads of belonging

Running away

I am running away again.

On my ballet toes I can just about reach the pink backpack.

The woman grown-up keeps putting it back up high. But there's no stopping me.

I call her Mummy. It's what the small one whines at her all day long.

Mummy smells like baby sick and strawberries.

Strawberries and sick, they are like a plait in my brain.

Mummy is the bag enemy.

Every morning, after Weetabix, I pack.

In go my Christmas slippers. It is cold on the outside. Next, jelly babies; six eggy-yoke, yellow ones and a royal purple one, just for luck. I borrow them from the jar next to the tiny one's bed.

Then squeeze in my book; 'An A to Z of Redcar'.

A man called Pete had a red car once. Shiny red on the outside it was. Seats on the inside; the colour of Cornish ice cream.

A cardboard tree hung from its silver mirror. It smelt like a Flower Show rose.

In the zippy pocket I put a necklace that Pete gave me. The beads are the colour of holiday sea. That holiday I had strappy shoes with no toes. I wore my flowery swim-thing all day long. A voice in the radio sang 'Itsy bitsy'. Pete twisted the knob and winked.

With my treasures packed, I am ready.

I could make a run for it anytime of course. Nimble- that's me.

A free spirit, he'd say, grabbing me round the middle.

But then Mummy will make me take a nap.

A nap? In the middle of the day!

Everyday!

Will that girl ever learn?

When I wake up, the backpack is always back up high; high and empty.

She's the rug well and truly pulled out from under me this time.

I'd stay here really, if it wasn't for the rules.

So Many Rules

Eat this. Drink that. Nap now. Do you need to pee?

I always need to pee. Sometimes I already have.

Mummy's face feels sad when I touch it then. The skin above her eyebrows crinkles like the old, shed roof we had. The one attached to our red bricked semi. That house on the High Street.

I'm taking no chances today.

It's nap time. I twist the fluffy handles tight. Squeeze my special belongings under my chin. Clamp shut my eyes. Nap.

Oh, but she comes into the room sudden. The air sputters from her mouth like a wet birthday balloon.

Mam, Mam, will you ever stop taking Lucy's new backpack?

Tomorrow's her first day of school.

That mummy one, she sounds a bit broken.

Her hands are gentle and familiar. I watch as they peel back wrinkled fingers from rose coloured straps. She looks down at me with Pete's blue eyes.

Maybe I won't run away today.

Derry Peace Bridge - under construction

With passion

Dreamers built a concept

Chin stroking creatives blueprinted me in each direction

Sporting sunshine yellow hard hats

Khaki and camo nowhere in sight.

With determination

Engineers swung me high

flipped me back, stretched me to

The Other Side

An act of faith they struggled to believe

With vigour

Construction workers skimmed the pockmarks riddling my banks

Smoothing over my fractured past

Ensuring speeding cyclists

No longer endured a bumpy ride.

With flourish

Finishers dotted my tarmac

With ancient buff brass oak leaves

Their crinkled edges marking out a path

For exhausted tourists with Troubles overload.

With time

I grew up beautiful

My snaking arc a curved streak of hope

Spanning the centuries' divide

City optimism spilling over petunia crazed planters

Each January, on a night that bites

A dignified father walks my span.

Navigating the serpent curves

Focusing his old, angry anguish

on the swirling water dashing below me

Each heavy hearted step he takes

Jangles my freshly taut nerves.

Both of us tingling with the itch of the scars

Just beneath my shiny hope-filled surface

Contact lenses demonstration: Ten easy steps.

1. Agree that your face would indeed look younger and happier without, what your partner refers to as, your 'Bottle bottoms'.

2. Allow said partner to book your appointment at a time convenient to you both - a timelapse after New Year, a few days before Valentine's.

3. Relax a little when you discover the optician is both old and unattractive. Relax even more when he offers your fella a hard, plastic seat straddling the corridor.

4. Try hard not to wince as the portly ophthalmist guides your arm over your head. Maybe yesterday's ribs have not quite healed, but making a fuss will not be appreciated.

5. Hold your upper eyelid open and back. Avoid the white ridge of skin where last Halloween's steri-strip stuck.

6. Refuse to be triggered as you poke yourself in the eye with your shaky, middle finger. It was only

that once and afterwards you were reminded it takes two to tango.

7. Giggle a little, but not too long or too loud, when the white coated eye-guy comments that you seem a little tense.

8. It is possible he'll suggest you seem somewhat awkward with your hands. Smile whilst hearing 'cack-handed, more like' muttered from the corridor. Grin manically as your ineptitude is labelled.

9. Stare hard at your Specsavers saviour. If (and this is crucial) your stare is pleadingly successful, he will ask you if you feel alright. With luck he will mention that people often get 'woozy' at this first fitting. *Some*, he may say, looking kindly into your watery eyes, glancing to the corridor and back, *some even faint*.

10. FAINT

At the hospital Louise reassured the familiar and weary paramedic she would be making a statement this time. Adamant, as she was, that she could see clearly now.

Jimmy Kerr

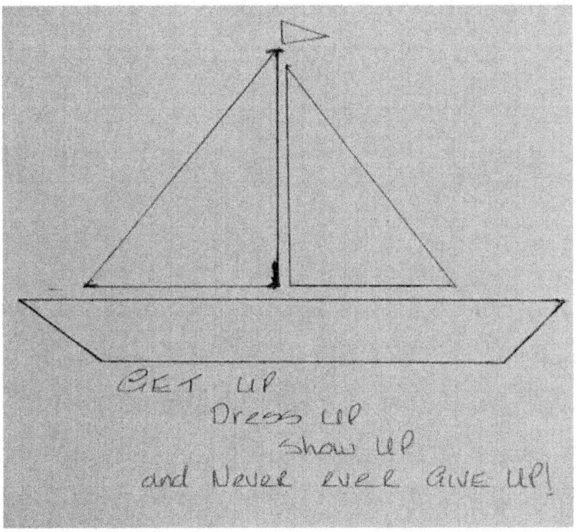

Jimmy Kerr is a writer/performer. His internationally produced play *Ardnaglass on the Air* was last staged at the Lyric, Belfast in 2017 and had a subsequent regional tour. He has performed, produced work in the Origins 1st-Irish festival in NY on four separate occasions, and is the recipient of the Origin Award for Special Achievement. During his time in Edinburgh, Kerr collaborated with the *Edinburgh International Science* festival on their touring show *Day or Night. Giant Productions*, the Glasgow based, children's arts development organization commissioned Kerr on three separate occasions to write and perform work. He was shortlisted for the *Abbey Works 2019,* and long listed for *Papatango* 2020. His first work of fiction was published in the 2022 winter edition of the international literary journal, *Trasna*. The same work was a Winner of the 2023 *Impspired Soundwaves Competition,* which he performed at the subsequent *Showcase Event*. Jimmy Kerr is a graduate of the Professional Actor Training program at the William Esper Studio in NYC, and holds a Masters in Creative Writing from the University of Edinburgh.

George's

Multiple laminated sheets offer substance and sustenance to animated diners of distinction in all shapes, sizes, ages, colour at George's on 57th and 5th.

Black coffee arrives first, scalding, perfectly bitter.

Parents discuss a child who's having issues at school, only to be interrupted by a man who recognises the mother. Turns out they went to the same school, used to sit beside each other and haven't seen each other since the age her daughter is now. The woman's face turns from despair to hope.

Home fries, crispy bacon, white toast, grape jelly, two eggs over easy show up. Time for a refill.

Two elderly neighbours check-in. Kids are throwing eggs at her house. Ideas and solutions shared. She called the cops already. "You don't need this excitement at your age". "Are you kidding me, I love the excitement". I take my check, tip well for the food but especially the entertainment. I miss this place. Everything and nothing has changed in ten years.

Angry Chicken

I mean is it chicken? If it's chicken, when was it chicken or even a chicken?

I'm sitting in a fried chicken outlet on Bedford Square sucking a carbonated syrup drink from a paper cup and I notice what looks like lipstick on the straw tip. I took the bait and upsized to a large soda and fries for 99 pence. I don't want either, I'm not hungry anymore but what is way worse, is, three hours ago I was forty-one days sober.

The time from a chicken entering a broiler house until leaving for slaughter is forty-two days.

Rather than congratulate Ian and sour the line of happy faces begging for a personalised scribble in the new book, *his best so far*. I left after the talking, before the additional hugging and free drinking. Everything was oh so cliche happy! Happy for Ian and his oh so well-deserved success. Happy to just be in a room with handsome Ian, because he's that to. Ian and the wine, and the home-made shortbread in the shape of swans that his two dads baked for him. I bet that made them happy. Happy to be doing that for their only child, a son with his eighth book in ten years and his one year of sobriety. A double celebration, a treble if you consider that the uninvited, miserable shadow in the room, me, didn't stick around for the shortbread distribution.

And here I am, lip bleeding tucking into a bargain bucket for one. Picking seasoned chicken from blackened bones as two foreign nationals berate and tear strips of each other at the table by the door. I have no context of what this irate man is roaring at this solid woman. Whatever's going on, it's being permitted, ignored even, but it's most definitely going on and he, for certain, is a horrible man.

Two girls at a nearby table, who might be known to or from the same place as the irate couple, watch with fascination seemingly understanding what is being roared in this otherwise calm space. I am the outsider. Anger rises within and rotates around me in this horrible room with horrible music and horrible chicken that I can't eat or enjoy. I sip and bleed and wonder where or how it happened. So, I stop trying to stem the flow.

Getting up to leave the American chicken franchise in the middle of Bedford square on a wet and grey evening, I stare straight through the man who humiliated the woman and is now berating someone else on his iPhone. Maintaining eye contact I dump my drink, tray and stolen, unsigned copy of Ian's eighth self-help book, titled *Swan*, into the garbage. I want the irate man to know that what he did to that woman, what he's doing right now as he stares me straight in the eye, is not okay and that if he wants to start something in this near empty restaurant, in this exact moment his nose, skull, or his lip will bleed in Bedford square.

And all because I asked a bartender with overbleached brittle hair,

"Harp or Guinness? Lager or stout?"

Then I ask what's her best seller. She tells me "Smithwick's" but that's not a lager or a stout I protest.

She's been bartending for years she tells me, yet while holding a pint glass that says Harp on the side, she's just had the realisation that Harp is lager. That's not good enough. I am disputing your intelligence and the strength of the peroxide that has saturated your skull. I didn't ask about your hairstyle, but you feel the need to tell me you did it yourself. I neither congratulate nor commiserate, but I worry that you may have got the measurements wrong when you can't get the card machine to work, and you can't decide to accept card or cash. My phone pings, you got there. You have done your job. I was just making conversation in this empty bar where I used the toilet and felt obliged to talk on the way out even though I asked permission first. And now, here I am sitting at a table, staring out across the street at flashing red neon lights coming from a chicken restaurant, with a pint of Harp in an empty bar on a Monday night in Bedford Square, wondering why I did that. I know exactly why.

A seed has been planted. Cold beer and salty fried chicken. I should know better.

I haven't written in months. I have started reading three books in the past month, and last week I signed up to a website where I can sell books I have or haven't read. I have still to post anything to my account.

"How's your Harp?" blondie asks.

I don't know. All I know is that I'm going to a book launch, and I'll probably grab something to eat after. I haven't eaten all day. I know that there is possibly one book in me which has yet to be titled or indeed written. Ian has written his eighth book and despite not having read it, I know I am in it. He's a writing writer. Despite my deepest wishes there is chicken that just doesn't taste like chicken. There is anger where there should be happiness. There is emptiness where there should be substance. Nothing is what it seems.

Two people were arrested in an American fried chicken outlet on Bedford Square that night.

Michaela McDaid

Without formal education in writing, Michaela Mc Daid needed the courage of middle age to pursue her literary ambitions. Life events and circumstances that once restricted her have become a powerful driving force.

Michaela has published articles and essays in local and national press and written and recorded poetry for BBC Radio. She has performed her writing to audiences at numerous events, including filming at the Playhouse Theatre, Derry, and has published short stories in three anthologies and poetry in one.

As an Impspired Soundwaves finalist for her short story in 2023, Michaela went back to the Competition Showcase a year later to win the Best Performance Trophy. As well as international publication of a personal essay in 2024, she continues to work hard on a novel that used to be a memoir, but changed its mind.

As a 'late starter' Michela believes she always had a strong voice, she just needed to clear her throat.

Stay!

Drawn down
held tight
made stay

leaden limbs
treacle air

I melt like wax
seep into earth

Each raindrop
plants me deeper

My body
not my own
consumed

a power
thick and visceral
absorbed in every cell

returning, slowly
to where I was
before this world

Time
expands, shrinks, dissolves

Back to human circle
in a bubble
separate, heavy
different

Body shapes blurred
voices distorted

Can not comprehend
Can not speak
words won't form

surrender
to be released

Edges

At the edge
I pause
for permission

in reverence to all living here

liminal space
elemental meeting place
of land and sea and air

bone and blood and breath
is all I am
in your embrace

I move with ease
home and lost
held and free

a rhythmic dance
you lead

I follow

rise and fall
ebb and flow

connected cycles
of push and pull

your patterns and power
reflected in me

being

in water
with water
like water

edges
dissolve

Mother Nature is an Irish Mammy and she's left you a voicemail

"Hellooo!
Hello, can you hear me?
It's me, your Mother, Nature.
Remember me?

Answering machine again!
I hate talking to machines,
and ye know I canni text.

How are ye love?
I haven't heard from ye in ages

You were far better at keeping in touch during the pandemic.
Aaah, we spent some quality time together then.
But now you've speeded up again,
you're busy, distracted,
no time for me.

I miss you
And we need to talk
It's just wile hard to get your attention

I do try

I whisper in the wind,
I roar in the waves
And I sing the sweetest birdsong

But you don't hear me,
because you're not listening

I still provide everything you need - naturally,
but now you have artificial heat, artificial light,
artificial food and medicine
you think you don't need me at all any more

but you do
you need me now,
more than ever

But you just take me for granted

Ach, I know you're still evolving,
but you're getting too big for your synthetic man-made boots.

I remember when you were a young species
we did everything together then
you appreciated me, and listened to my wisdom
back when we were close.

Other animals still know my worth
and stay close to me,
it's just you that we seem to have lost.

You can't do it on your own love
I know you think you can
but you can't

We’re all still connected
We’re family.
We need each other

I especially miss the wee ones
and they miss me too,
even if they don’t realise it’s me that they’re missing

You don’t let them close enough to climb trees or dig dirt.
They don’t feel fresh air on their wee faces
‘cause they’re locked up in boxes,
heads bowed to screens.

Some of them are even scared of me,
because they don’t know me at all.

I don’t want to be angry
especially now, when you’re not well.
I feel your stress and sadness
and I want to soothe you
but you won’t come close enough to let me.

Even when you are with me, you’re not really present.
I’m just a nice background for your photos

You pixilate my beauty,

filter my perfection
and upload my wonder.

Our time together is all over in the push of a button,
as if you were never here at all.

You don't just be you,
being with me.

My health's not good
my temperature's rising
pollution has given me a wile cough
and my veins and arteries are clogged up with plastic.

I'm sick darling,
but I'm still strong.

We'll both get better,
we'll heal - together.
And when we do,
let's never lose touch again.

Come home to me love
for your own sake
and mine

With love,
Your Mother, Nature"

Treading the boards - Quietly

"Mammy, Mammy, I'm gonni be Mary!" I shout it out loud, running across the garden. It's the best news ever in my whole life. I pull the front door open hard and nearly trip, 'cause my feet can't keep up with me.

Mammy's sitting at the kitchen table wearing her blue cleaner's uniform; blue trousers and a shirt with dark patches under the arms. She's writing in her book with a pen in one hand and fag in the other. Mammy always writes in her book, but nobody ever knows what she's writing about. She quickly puts her fag in the ashtray and turns to face me with her legs and arms open, so I can run straight into the middle of her.

She smells like smoke and coffee. I jump up and down, tapping her legs, "mind how I told you we're doing a nat-ivity play at school for Christmas? and that means we get to act out the story of the birth of baby Jesus, and we'll be up on stage in the big hall, and the *whole* school, and *all* the Mammys and Daddys, and everybody in the whole town will come to watch us?" Big breath.

"Yes, Aisling love, you told me all about it, many times." She nods and smiles.

"And mind how I said I wanted to be Mary, 'cause she's very important 'cause she's Jesus's Mammy?"

"Yes, love" Mammy holds my hands together in hers.

"I got picked! I'm going to be MARY!"

"Ach Aisling, I'm delighted for you. That's great news, so it is".

I tell her all about it, "Today at school, we all had to read nice and loud, and Mr Doherty stayed at the very back of the class to make sure he could still hear us. Then he picked who would play what part. Nobody gets to play Baby Jesus, 'cause he's only a brand-new baby that didn't even learn to talk yet, so he doesn't say anything. That's why we don't need a real person to be him. We'll just use a baby doll wrapped in a blanket like the olden days. And I'M Mary, so I get to hold him and sit right in the middle." Big breath. "Louis Fowler is Joseph so he walks beside me and stands behind me when I'm sitting down. And Paddy Mc Henry, Tim Mullan and Connor Doran are three wise men, and that's funny 'cause they're stupid boys really, and I'm smarter than all of them. But it's ok, it's called 'a play', so you don't really have to be like the person you're pretending to be." Big breath. "Kathy and Jo-Anne and some other weans are angels, they stand at the back and be quiet when they're not singing. Kathy says she likes that better. She doesn't want to be up on a stage where everybody can see you and hear you. But I do!"

Daddy puts his paper down and coughs. I didn't even know he was there. I spin round, "I'm Mary, Daddy! I got picked for the best part in the whole play, out of everybody". He leans forward in his chair. "I think I got picked because I'm the best reader, and I look like Mary too 'cause I'm very white and my eyes are blue, and that is what the Virgin Mary looked like. I've seen loads of pictures of her. And I think she was Irish too. And as well, I'm a good Mary 'cause I always go to mass and say all my prayers." Mammy and Daddy smile at each other. "Mary's very important because she looks after

Jesus until he's big enough to do miracles and cure leopard-sy."

"Well now, aren't you the clever girl? A star is born, eh? Don't forget yer ol' fella when you hit the big time." Daddy lifts his paper again and I run down to my room to practise holding a doll.

****

Next day, I walk home from school very fast, my feet are hard on the ground. I go straight into the house, down the hall and slam my bedroom door behind me. I fall hard on my bed and push my face into my pillow. I kick my legs and they bounce back up off the bed. The pillow gets hot and wet against my face. It's not fair! The door opens slowly. Mammy sits close to me with her hand on my back, "What's wrong Aisling? What happened love?" Her voice is soft.

My chest is tight, snotters go into my mouth. I lift my head a wee bit, and talk to the pink flowers on my pillowcase, "I don't get to speak!", my head falls back down again.
"What do you mean love? You speak all the time, you've never been shy"
I lift my head again and keep looking at the pink flowers, they're blurry now. I say it slowly, "I don't get to speak when I'm Mary!"

Mammy takes her hand off my back and moves over so I can sit up. I swing my legs round and grab my school bag off the floor. I get the stupid script out of my bag, open it on my knees, and quickly turn the first page, then the next one, and the next one. "Look! Mary doesn't get to speak in the whole nativity play. Not even one single word! Joseph speaks, the stupid wise men speak . . . even the sheep says 'baaa.' But Mary doesn't say anything the whole time. She just holds the baby while all the boys do the talking. She's the most important one in the whole story, if it wasn't for her, there'd be no Jesus, and no story at all. But she just sits there, smiling, and looking nice."

With her arm round my shoulder, Mammy takes big breath, and wipes my tears.

"Ach I know darlin'. It's just the way of the world. People that should be heard, have no voice. And you're right, it's not fair!"

Seamus McDermott

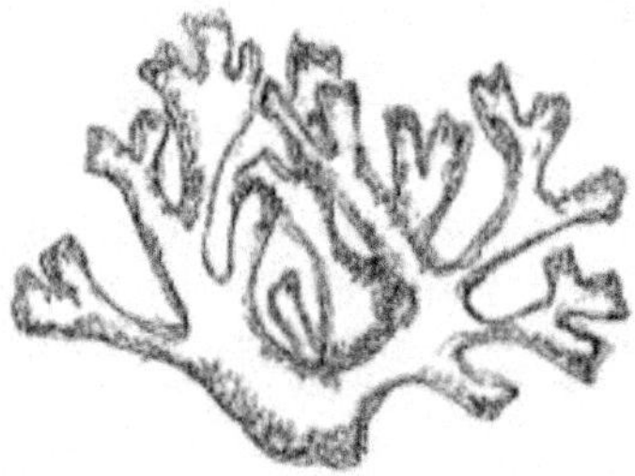

~ by Mary McDermott ~

Cold-water coral from
one thousand meters deep

Raised and living in the northwest of Ireland, Seamus Mc Dermott is an active member of '*The Diamond Writers*' and '*This Writing Thing*'. He enjoys writing poems influenced by nature and memories.
Seamus' video-poem '*Borderland*' was selected for screening at five international film festivals 2021-2023 and was the winner in Best Spoken Word/Poetry, *Miracle Makers International Film Festival* in 2023.

He was also the Frances Browne Literary Competition Winner of the '*Local Writer Award*', 2023, and the '*Treasure Each Voice Award*', 2024 with highly commended poems in 2021 and 2022. In the *Bangor Literary Journal Forty Words Competition*, he was shortlisted in 2021 and runner-up in 2022, as well as being an *Impspired Soundwaves Competition* Winner, 2024.

In the *Allingham Arts Poetry Competition*, he was highly commended in 2023 and shortlisted in 2020-2022. His poems were published in *Corncrake Magazine* 2023, *Honest Ulsterman* 2023, *The Madrigal Literary Magazine* 2022, *Hidden Donegal* anthology of Donegal poets 2022, *Little Gems Magazine* Spring, Summer, Autumn and Winter editions (2019 –2023), 11th edition of *Crossways Literary Magazine* 2021 and *The Bangor Literary Journal* issues 15 and 18.

Boathouse

Steering a trembling hand to the whiskey glass,
tillered shoulders caulked in a tweed jacket of seaweed
browns. His ebbing blue eyes horizon-ed at the end
of the bar counter. Warp and weft of dying ivy hold

up drystone walls, and lobster pots buttress the leeward
side of his boathouse, leaning into the wind at the end
of a small slipway. Fingers rust stained from cigarette
smoke rowlock-ed around his whiskey glass, unseize

cast iron hinges as they bleed a burnt orange upon
a creeping shadow from a tall icehouse. Whiskey
reclaims a dry cracking slipway as the tide recedes
from his dry chapped lips. Through a slipping slate

roof a shaft of light punctures a hole in his crumbling boat. Tides flood and ebb, ticks from his pocket watch anchored by a slack chain to a small pier in his mind. He always had sight of the shoreline, but now his crew all gone, he's cast adrift alone in unchartered waters.

My Grandfather

My Grandfather bled into the burnt
rust of his corrugated tin shed,
swallowed up by the tree trunk post,
burying his feet in the dirt floor.

Protruding from his worn, oil-soaked workbench,
the swirly unmovable knots, his thoughts.

Sharpened sword-like, his wooden-handled
hedge clipper blades, his wit.

Rattling inside his old biscuit tins,
the nuts, bolts and washers, his practical jokes.

Standing steady his tall metal locker, filled
with old iron tools, his stature.

Bolted firmly to his workbench, strong
iron vices, his hands.

Buried in a bundle of his brushed cotton
bedsheet rags, his warmth.

Trapped in his unfinished hidden naggin
of Irish whiskey, his worries.

Dinted and scraped into his rust-stained
tobacco tins, his words.

Lying redundant his unbolted gearbox
under the bench and bleeding oil, his heart.

grandfather oak

stands on the fringes

of the school playground

Autumn leaves flow from his heart

high in branches magpies   oily black   bright white

fight   squabble   skip   hop

roots running deep

under skipping feet

branches p l a y and s w a y   in dappled shadow

summer holiday

standing   in silence

loneliness settles

deep   into   bark   branch   twig   root

he fell in pain

tree surgeons slice and cut   until

nothing is left

children return

saplings   from the acorn's oak

arms   s w a y   p l a y

in the Autumn breeze

skip   hop

fight   squabble

dappled shadow memories

scattered   leaves

feathers   in their hair

sawdust   in their pockets

sap   in their veins

children without   a grandfather

Our Last Embrace

My heart, a floating buoy, cast adrift
on the ebbing tide. Our last words
pushed ashore on bow waves, smashing

upon the sharp granite rocks. Your smile
puppet-ed away by Arctic terns. Conversations
dissolving in the foam wake trailing behind

the boat. You silently squeezed my hand,
our last embrace carried away on the wings
of a cormorant flatlining across the horizon.

Under stained deck-boards,
among oily ballast stones,
bled your scalpel-ed heart.

Mark McGrath

A Derry man with Donegal as a mistress, Mark's love of the written word comes from the fantasy novels of his teens. Each of those stories opened a lifesaving door into other worlds which let him escape his depression. Mark has spoken about his journey of recovery at *Tenx9* events and more recently on behalf of a mental health charity. He has a soft spot for the literary dark arts of Cormac McCarthy, particularly Blood Meridian, Child of God and The Road.

Austerity

The parasitic finger
points a whisper at its weak
It severs doe eyed pennies' trust
with every word we speak
I'm harmed in hearing voices
sick or fallow   claiming hope
When children starved
of thoughtless choices
can't afford to cope

They drink and smile and waver
all as futures in the wind
They practice smiles much simpler
salivating gaping grins.
Is it an opportunist claim
to want a right to rule
As widows weep for mercy
in the ghost of failing schools?

Rote learning is the whip
the whipper's throat to hold first place
As infants disappear
their tears will find no hiding place
inside a world of faces down
from seeking pence
they beg to feed
the dire outstretch of weeping voices
in the huddle of their seed

Bang incest in the breaking of the ranks
to warp our kind
no kindly thought salvation
nor a socio-stable bind
We come apart   he whimpers
as it slithers off the ledge
The heart-blind pick
their flesh to bone
and burn their paper pledge

I once was them   an infant
tearful hope and cuddle warm
I looked out to the future
knelt in lies to feed their charm
A Christ rock litter passage
zombie mind to murk in hate
The ritual of our downfall
is this failure of a state

The murk I am once had a mother
who defiled its want for love
Sold the stretch of studied blubber
to the jailor down above.
Cried and crucified   tectonic
left to shudder from the grave
Prayer is clichéd revolution
Every child is born a slave

To live in memory of stories
that a happy ending mocks
The rotting poverty of teeth
and corn starch syrup death of shock
Deserving poor and failing soil steps
out of trusted granite mind
The hate will carry our survival
to decapitate their kind

The window closes like a coffin
on a home that cannot heat
The furtive dirt of shivered fathers
doomed in shadows at the meet
They sell each other grumbled wisdom
Lack of action in the press
Empty talk of revolution
in their infantile regress

Boor connected to the damage
of a privileged bitter few
The curséd victims of a government
whose lies are nothing new
There is a clarity in fear
that keeps the people in their place
Until we answer with a bullet
we will drown in our disgrace

The bullet difference is a battle ring
A shrill escape from black

A sharp and pointed song of limits
Sung to auger fighting back
The lyric taught to sleeping children
To awaken and prepare
We will own this weeping Eden
We will make the bastards care

The window closes like the hope
that owns a coffin full of men
A world of fathers in the flesh
and collared poverty descends
In vowing scripture of the figment
of oppressing female lives
Conserve the truth in clenched fist
struggle
as the wisdom flower dies

Carry On

A tiny life lay stuck in the soil at my feet. Rolled back on its shell, it kicked out in soft chaos like a new-born baby. A gust of wind had felled the little creature. Struggling between the stones.

Noticing my shadow, it froze. Fate was hovering overhead, a silent cloud swallowing its sky. It was oblivious to how brief its journey would be through the turbulent passage of time.

My neglected fingernails. They could softly nudge its fragile form the way my little Becca used to. The way she still does when I dream. But I am afraid to nudge. Terrified to dream.

Sometimes I wake in fear and scream. The morning burns its cheery creed into the sockets of my skull. The cruel contorted cull of sleep in birdsong breaches darkness, steals her ghost. Reveals her empty room, the toys she loved the most. The lie in her belief that she would never hurt a fly.

The frozen loneliness of grief. A clouded eulogy in dreams. The struggle not to read her name carved into stone. The disbelief. Her end date breathed into my bones. The hours that I pretend to cope. The endless seconds that I don't.

The insect wrestled with its weight. It put a tiny leg against a stone. It almost saved its fate. It struggled and fell back. It was not meant to make it home. So it gave up its pointless struggle. I looked away to let it die alone.

"Dad?"

I put a fragile finger down to nudge it on. To help this tiny creature just enough to make it move along. And once it understood that I meant it no harm, it journeyed on. And like that, it was gone. She was gone.

I stared up into the silent sky and froze. Then, I turned back from the cliff edge to make my weary journey home. Because I felt the softest nudge to move myself enough to carry on alone.

They come in waves

In sleepless nights and rubber boats

the huddled eyes and crumbled notes

of former lives

the angels wait

to hear their sobs and indicate

how close to shore

the smugglers curse

where mothers weak with hunger nurse

their beacon young

until the seers' silent search

for lights appear

The cradled hush begins to drown

when hunger

makes a helpless sound

The Boundary

breached

alarm of noise

a seer grabs a sobbing boy

and casts him in the violent surf

to give his screaming lungs

the girth of death's great liquid pacifier

bound to join the silence down

in silt and bones as old as grass

where feed the fish this flesh and glass

to scuff and dim for hollow ends

of stolen souls when life pretends

at more than broken hope

for those

whose fathers feel

the hostile prose

of politicking privileged men

whose currency in hate

defends a poverty

in threatened ears

fed fear

as brown diseases near
on every boat
that begs the shore
of failure fathers
wanting more
than surf and violence
for their young
their futures lost
the seas become
the naked lack of choice they brave
men praying foreign gods will save
a life preserver for their boys
in chaos on the thresh of noise

We build the West a wall of shore
They try to climb it wanting more
Than silent endings for their young
Before their dreams of hope become ...

Words Inc

A Writers Group, at first in 2022 facilitated by the Northern Ireland Library Authority, now independent and meeting weekly in the Town Hall in Coleraine, Northern Ireland

Ian Garner *~ collator ~*

Ian's interest in creative writing was sparked by an invitation to join a local Writers' Circle, back in the 1990s, when living in England. On moving to Northern Ireland in 2001, he continued to develop his interest in creative writing while pursuing his scientific and business career, until retirement in 2022. On joining the Coleraine-based writing group, Words Inc, the same year, Ian has since written prose and poetry, some of which was published in *Sea Spray and Woodland Glades*, an Anthology featuring writers from the North Coast of Ireland, published by Impspired Press in 2024.

Memory Fades

Did we cavort on sun-blanched sands
along strand lines
revelling in the warm Azores breath   pushing onshore?

Were there chases among the dunes
slithering down-slope   scrambling to tops
the race never run?
diverse encounters with kindred souls
sometimes strangers   soon-to-be friends.

Your nascent wisdom growing
young life embracing rituals that excited and pleased
until Summer waned   as did you

How could this joy of being
sweet
enriching
unconditional
be taken from you?

What taboo was broken   demanding such payment?
Nature   without conscience
relentless   replacing

Stripped back matter   motes
fleeting impostors as thoughts
my memory of you
is beginning
to fade.

October 4th

Memory

Sky blue day

Tide wave surf

Eternal

Laugh skip prance

Bond sing dance

Backward glance

Memory

Footnote: A Snám Suad is an eight-line Irish poem and/or stanza. All lines have 3 syllables with the following rhyme pattern: aabcdddc. Lines four and eight are 3-syllable words, all other lines end in monosyllabic words

Prague prologue

Hannah watched him, watching them. The Watcher, perched on the rough edge of a concrete bench, bespectacled, tousled black hair, eyes squinting in late-September sunshine. Leaning forward, hands palm down on the seat, feet crossed, tucked under, mouth agape, he made furtive glances left, towards them; a couple sat alongside. Her back to the Watcher, the young woman leant towards her companion, their heads close, speaking, laughing.

From her nearby vantage point, perched on a low wall, sun behind her, she kept them in view. Her mission, to photograph the Watcher. Rolleiflex strap slung around her neck, camera held steady, she angled its lens towards them. Oblivious to the thrum of Letná Park she looked down at the image inverted in the viewfinder, adjusting, framing her target. The Watcher, restive, was pulling at his tan overcoat now mottled with dark smears, smooth from constant wear. He touched a folded magazine set in an outer pocket before again settling his black fingers, stark against pale concrete, over the front edge of his seat. She paused and re-framed.

Camera steady, shutter release taut, she looked up, glancing sideways at them, waiting for a gap in the crowd.

Click.

Across the river, church bells rang for Evening Mass. Rising, the couple blended with the stream of visitors heading towards Czech bridge. The Watcher, gaze continuing, transfixed, leant further forward, swinging his legs from under, propelling himself into a slow, shuffling walk to follow. Hannah framed another shot to capture his pursuit.

She stood and merged with the bridge-bound exodus, and while walking, in one well-practised movement, she rewound the film, unclipped the camera back with her right thumb, tipped the film canister into her left palm before flipping it shut. Two fingers of her clenched left hand pulled back the flap of her satchel resting on her left hip to slide her hand inside, releasing the canister into a waiting white paper bag before twisting the neck of the bag closed. She was ready.

Heart racing, excitement, and fear sparring for supremacy, she lifted the bag dropping it into a waste basket by the exit, telling herself,

Don't look back.

The Watcher had marked Hannah, looping back, shadowing.

Her tram to central Prague pulled away, sunset-orange streaks flickering off its grimy windows. She saw the Watcher reach into the waste basket. White bag in hand, rising, he looked in her direction and smiled. Then she glimpsed the young couple by the gates. Tram accelerating, stretching to look back, she watched them, watching him, watching her.

Frankie Bradley

Hailing from New York City, Frankie packed their bags and moved away to pursue a doctorate in creative writing at Ulster University in Northern Ireland. They specialize in fantasy prose but enjoy dabbling in poetry when they find the right subject. You can find them breaking down and analyzing video game narrative every other Thursday on their podcast, *Reignite* (found wherever fine podcasts are sold). *Changeling* was first published in *Writing from the Heart*, an anthology collated by Jae Jenkins Scott and Robbie Taylor and published by *Impspired*, 2025. *Escape Into the Stars* was first published in *Paperclip Vol 4,* an anthology published by Ulster University in 2024. Also, they foster cats and hobbies as needed.

Changeling

I didn't understand when I saw you in our mother's arms. No one told me that you would be here, pink and wrinkled under fluorescent lights. She held you with tender arms. Did she ever hold me that way? I can't remember. Maybe she knew she wouldn't get to hold you for long.

Another woman—another mother—swept you up into her arms that night while we were supposed to be asleep. What I thought was a scrap of shadow, a fragment cast by car headlights that sped by my open window, shifted and moved against the light in a way that made me squeeze my eyes tight. All I remember are flashes through partially opened lids—the woman made of darkness lifting you from your crib, her forehead pressed against yours, tears of starlight dripping onto your pale moon face. Then: nothing. You were gone.

Later, when I try to tell your story, to make sense of this fragment of my life, no one would believe me. Even our parents called me a liar. They told me you didn't exist. You never existed. The memory of you drifted to the bottom of the sea in my mind, covered in murk and sediment, impossible to excavate unless you already knew it was there.

Those Left Behind

Of course Cinderella gets a fairy godmother. Beauty wasn't enough? A neck as graceful as a swan's, skin softer than velvet, and an arsenal of magic... that she used for what? A pretty dress and a man who could only lay claim to her by her feet?

Our mother was terrible to her, I'll admit. We know this. But what about *me*? I saw how the wind was blowing but I chose to survive. So what if that meant being a bitch to my only sister? It meant I wouldn't be the target. In our house it was kill or be killed.

When I look up at the moon I wonder if there's a godmother out there for me. I wouldn't ask for a gown or a coach or anything so fleeting. I'd ask for a horse which ran like wildfire. I would ride far, far away, where my mother's corsets can no longer squeeze me, her makeup brushes can no longer abrade my skin. I could be free.

Tonight the moon is a sliver – orange and warm like a citrus grin. I hear my mother crooning to her patchwork cat, the only creature she'd never criticize. Cinderella used to look up at the moon like this. With a kingdom laid at her dainty feet, I suppose she never needs to look up again.

I guess there is no magic remaining for those left behind.

The Moon

The moon was a plain depth, uncomplicated in its distance. It was an orb without question, no mystery attached. We took it for granted in our night sky, a constant hoop of silver silk. It was simple, then. We were simpler people with no legend or lore. There was only the moment; there was only the moon.

The moon is a quizzical trim. It borders our sky with questions. We never had questions before but now they fill the sky like starlight, radiating from a beacon of curiosity. We are drawn to her now, seeking her out when she is at her fullest. We feel her colour in our edges with soft moonglow.

The moon will become an economic wedge. As our buildings rise higher to lift the rich above the smog and smoke, they will be able to see her face wax and wane while we see only bleak clouds roiling between us and the sky. We had so many questions, once. We used to be trimmed in curiosity, but now that is only for *them*. They will stand on their glass terraces, above the dirt and dark and poor, and savour that silver gift. But they will ask no questions.

Footnote:
This piece was inspired by the podcast Imaginary Advice by Ross Sutherland, episode 49 RE: The Moon

Escape into the Stars: A Tribute to Nex Benedict

Part One:

heroes become embedded in the stars

so it's no surprise to find you there

shining in defiance

your light refusing to dim

it burns across galaxies

until those that brutalized you into this celestial immortality

are nothing but dust

and the memory of you is triumphant

Part Two:

how can the peace you were forced into

be considered a gift?

the peace you deserved was meant to be *softer*

you should have had art school, covered in glitter, found family seated around a coffee stained table at 3am you deserved the peace of a life well lived

you deserved to grow into a person who could shake the world just as easily as they shook themselves from a nap

gentle peace

the peace of a life fully lived

Part Three:

I promise to write a world in which defiance is not met with disproportionate violence

I promise to read everything I can about you, books you'd have loved, the obituaries of those in our community who continue to fall with no one to protect them

I promise to try to hold it together, try things that scare me, try to stand up for myself and others

I promise to dream a better future, dream *my* life fully lived

I promise to make art, make scarves and sweaters that hug my loved ones close, make knitted flowers to keep spring alive all year, never *stop* making

I promise to make my life bigger and better.

Part Four:

I came out as non-binary at 30.

I came out as pansexual at 25.

At 16, I knew I was queer, but I didn't know the words.

I was bullied, but never beaten.

I was lucky.

What if I came out sooner?

Could it have been me in that hospital bed?

Who would have taken the brutal swing that battered my head against the ground?

My father? My classmates?

Me?

Desperate for escape as I was … what if they made it worse until I only saw one way out

A narrow tunnel, void of pinpricks of light to guide my way.

Nex is woven into everything I do, every word I write

It could so easily have been me

I was lucky

I *did* escape.

I found my way to the stars.

Rita Doherty

For seven decades, Rita Doherty has lived in Ballymena, *City of Seven Towers*, in Northern Ireland, apart from two years in London. A medical and legal secretary in London, Ballymena, and Belfast, after early retirement she joined various Creative Writing Groups, writing prose, poetry, scripts and has even dabbled in song writing, all inspired by her life experiences and holidays abroad.

In the Creative Writing world, Rita chaired the Braid Centre Writers' Group for two years introducing differing types of creative writing. She particularly enjoyed inviting local Northern Irish writers Gerard McKeown, a slam poet, Gerry Miller and Paul Maddern, to attend the Group as guest tutors.

She has read her short stories, a poem *'Reiki'* and one of her scripts, *'Deceitful Diane',* in the Braid Centre in Ballymena, Northern Ireland. These were later published in various local anthologies. When her local hospital closed, Rita's tribute poem *'Ode to Waveney'*, was published in the *Ballymena Guardian* newspaper. In 2022 a piece entitled *'Nigerian Tea Ideas'* was published in the booklet *'You and Me'* issued by Northern Ireland Libraries.

Rita enjoys the challenge of composing poems and prose, receiving guidance from tutors and sharing knowledge and laughs with fellow class members. She is presently happily attending Words Inc , a Mary Farrell-led Coleraine Creative Writing Group

The Lorry, the bridge and the train

Bridge loomed ahead

Lorry sped along

Central position chosen

Horrific scraping noise

Driver alarmed

Lorry jerked to a halt.

Horror hit, lorry was trapped

Cars passed cautiously

Horns blasting.

Lorry driver's pulse raced

Bridge damage unknown

Next train time unknown.

Emergency service arrived

Car drivers irate

Busy world screeched to a halt.

No one injured

All lived to see another day

Coleraine was abuzz with talk of

The lorry, the bridge and the train

Basement

I could delay no longer, I must investigate.

Creeping down the descending steps towards the basement, I tried to open the heavy wooden door, applying greater pressure when it moved. With a loud squeak, it gave way. The inward-opening door propelled me into darkness.

I felt around the walls for a light switch.

Reaching the end of a narrow corridor, colourful lights appeared around the room. A revolving globe of mirrored multi-coloured sparkling twinklers hung from the ceiling. Two music decks blasted melodies from the floor. Beautiful bodies danced around, moving their limbs in time to the tunes. I stood in amazement looking at the sight, feeling my toes starting to tap with the rhythm, getting used to the soft lighting and the happy atmosphere of the scene. The crowd beckoned me to join in; gingerly I moved forward.

I was soon swept along with the beat.

A neatly dressed waiter approached with a tray of drinks. Thirsty from the exertion, I accepted the liquor, all fears of accepting unknown beverages having disappeared. The glowing contents of the glass had a beautiful tangy taste. I gulped it down, wanting to rejoin the dancers. Beginning to wonder about the time, I pushed thoughts of work on the following day to the back of my mind.

Then I panicked. Wanting to escape, I raced to the door and struggled to open it, but it was locked. My screams for help were drowned out by the noise of the music.

I was trapped.

The music stopped, glaring lights disappeared, I was back in my bedroom. I had locked the door - was it all a dream?

The next morning as I left the house, I glanced towards the basement. There was no evidence of the previous night's rave. I will never have an explanation of what happened as I moved to another building on the following day, but I will never lose the memory of that night.

Ten Cygnets in the Park Dam

Proud parents took ten cygnets for a morning swim
In order to keep their small brood trim

One decided not to stay
the Good Lord took him away

One swallowed bait
that left eight

Two swirled into the 'Devil's Cup'
meaning *their* time was up

One took flight became
caught on a wire of light

wings flapped
neck snapped

In time three swans fully grown
from the dam had gone, had flown

leaving one lovely son with his mam
skimming together cross the glassy dam.

Maura Doran

BEE HAPPY

Originally from Armagh, Northern Ireland, Maura Doran now spends her time between Derry and Donegal. A former international performing arts examiner with Trinity College London, her work took her into the literary hubs of many countries. She was also an adjudicator for the Hong Kong Speech Festival and lead judge for the Shakespeare Competition, Sri Lanka. When in 2020 world travel was no longer possible, she rekindled her love of writing with the help of a bursary from the Irish Writer's Centre, Dublin by following various writing courses. Maura now holds an MA in Creative Writing from the Seamus Heaney Centre, Queen's University, Belfast, Northern Ireland. A member of two Northern Irish Writing Groups, *Words Inc* and *this writing thing* she is also a volunteer story reader for the Verbal Arts Centre, Derry.

MELTING...

Hands cupped around a hot coffee. Winter rain beats against the kitchen window creating an obscure watercolour. A blurred transformation of the beautiful North Coast landscape.

The lumpy old freezer is defunct. To move it, packed ice must be defrosted. Vinegar and hot water are ready for the congealed mass. But hot air is my true ally for this task.

The white noise of the hair dryer is hypnotising. I drift into a reverie - a mix of times past, things to do.

A large piece of ice drops, alerting me to the heavy onslaught of water. Thick towels are insufficient defence, and the brown tiled floor turns shiny, translucent. Observing the gathering speed of the melt, I hear the warning mantras of Attenborough and Thunberg.

We are hair dryers.

We are melting our ice caps.

Is the watery landscape, on a North Coast window, a portent of things to come?

Flushed Out

A jabbing pain exploded in Cora's mouth as she entered the staffroom of the local secondary school. The dentist had warned her the wisdom tooth would need to come out. In the meantime, Cora had to take antibiotics, three times a day, always with food.

Coward. Cora admonished herself, she should have had the damned thing out once and for all. But, hey, this way she had to eat three times a day. Diet - take a hike.

There was no sign of Zac, the new drama teacher. Unusual, he was always the first in for staff lunch. Always scrounging for treats. Always in first to raid others lunch boxes. Cora clicked on the full kettle. With her left hand cupped around her jaw, she lifted her mug from the cupboard. Pulling a teabag out of the caddy she lopped it into the gaping mouth of her red cup. Pouring out the hot water, glancing over to her shelf, even from here she could see that her chocolate energy bites had been tampered with.

Leaving the tea to brew she retrieved the plastic container to look inside. There should have been three, only one remained. She placed the box back on her shelf, a playful smile on her lips.

Zac wasn't his usual exuberant, dramatic self when he entered the staffroom. He was pale, moaning and hugging his stomach.

You okay? Asked Cora.

Not good. Zac bleated. *Feel awful, don't know what's wrong. Maybe a tummy bug.*

Can I get you tea or water? Enquired Cora.

Nope. Need to run.

Zac bolted for the door heading off in the direction of the staff toilets.

Cora chucked the uneaten energy bite into the bin. She washed out the container and placed it back on the shelf. Retrieving a fresh energy bite from her bag, she ate it before taking an antibiotic.

With a chuckle, she placed her antibiotics back into her bag, beside a packet of chocolate flavoured Super-Lax.

Happy little chap.

Right. I'll clear out this box, then I'll get a coffee. Sorting out old documents is not my forte. They grow in the dim and dusty environment of our loft - a bit like mushrooms. Last week, Woman's Hour had an article on the benefits of using the Marie Kondo method to declutter your home: keeping items which spark joy.

I prefer the William Morris approach: have in your house, only things which you believe to be useful, or, that you believe to be beautiful. For fun, I sometimes ask my husband if he is useful or beautiful? Should I keep him? By the way, he's both, so he stays.

Anyhow, Radio 4 gave me the kick start I needed to put order back into the mushroom department. One box before a coffee-break. Opening the lid, I saw it, stopping me in my tracks. Not a mouse or a spider, but a small yellow folded card with the sketched outline of a dog on the front, the words Dogs Trust emboldened on top. Outside, the edges frayed with age, inside the details written on his kennel board, that first time we saw him.

Name: Wotsit
Breed: Mixed
Age: Two
Character: Happy little chap. Chases cats. Gets on well with other dogs. Good with children.

I see the smiling faces of four excited children on our day out, off to the Dogs Trust - just for a look.
We take our time enjoying the company of the dogs, then note three favourites.

- *A black, short legged, fellow, perched high on an old armchair, big brown eyes, head tilting from side to side.*

- *A fluffy white westie, with a cheeky grin and bright eyes.*

- *A brindle coated whippet - one ear up, one ear down, prancing on long ballerina legs.*

We make our way to Reception, fingers crossed that one of these canine characters might suit our lively family. Each of us trying to contain our excitement.

- *The westie?*

- *Sorry, not great with kids. Really more suited to a calm, quiet environment.*

- *The whippet?*

- *Sorry, not a family dog, more suited to outdoors. Not fully housetrained yet. Still needs a lot of work.*

- *The black short legged fellow.*

.

- *Perfect for you guys. We were hoping you'd pick him; we'd matched him to you.*

Four sets of eyes focus on mine.
I look at them.
Four sets of eyes plead.
I nod, knowing he'll understand.

That evening. No need to explain. He knows me too well. When he heard that the kids and I were off to the Dogs Trust - just for a look - sure he knew what to expect.

The next weekend we returned to the Dogs Trust.

Wotsit.

We’ll always miss him.
Our happy little chap.
The box can wait.
I put his card into my pocket
I’ll read it again over coffee

Ruth Holloway

The town of Coleraine in Northern Ireland has been Ruth Holloway's home for over thirty years. She has been writing ever since she was a little girl. A member of two writing groups, *Words Inc* and a Zoom writing group, *The Procrastinators,* she prefers to write short stories.

Her inspiration comes from horror films, creepypasta, pangolins and cats. She is drawn to anything strange or mysterious such as Roald Dahl's *Tales of the Unexpected.*

Her short story *The Perfect Wedding Dress* was published in 2022 by *Impspired Press*. Also, five pieces of her work, *Dreamy Dave, Mr Big, The Lion, the Mouse and the Bird, Obsession,* and *The Child Capsule* feature in the Anthology *Sea Spray and Woodland Glades* published by *Impspired* in 2024.

Listen To Your Heart was first published *in Writing From the Heart*, an Anthology collated by Jae Jenkins Scott and Robbie Taylor, published by *Impspired* in 2025.

Found

I saw you   I walked away

with more strength than you expected

becoming whole again

you broke me but broke can be fixed

every day I mend

the more I stay away

the more I grow

I'm worth more than you paint me

You can act as if I don't exist

I can't pretend the same

My day moves on without you

as I fill the vacuum you left behind

I stretch my day with purpose

I stand with pride

I've found myself

at last

The Heart Doesn't Question

I still love you

the heart doesn't question why

I still care

the heart doesn't question how

eight years since you were mine

the heart doesn't question when

you were cruel   I was kind

the heart doesn't question reason

I want you back

the heart doesn't question that

but it should

Invisible Illnesses

Suffering every day in silence, I've had Irritable Bowel Syndrome since I was 17. In pain all the time, spasms and cramps give me no peace. I can never go far from a toilet as I have to go so often.

Starting to feel exhausted most of the time I spent most of my time resting in bed, also with pain in my legs and body. The doctors didn't know what it was but since my sister has fibromyalgia, they put it down to that. I found it hard to do activities I enjoyed as everything just exhausted me.

I've had depression since my teenage years. It tells me that life isn't worth living, that it's not worth doing anything, that my dreams will never come true. It also is another big reason why I just spend my time resting. I used to run onto the road because I was hoping to get knocked down, but thankfully I haven't done that in recent years. I also suffered such anxiety about going outside. I couldn't do it sometimes.

Due to Manic Psychosis I had to go into hospital for four months, where I had terrifying hallucinations about the end of the world. Curiously, I still have some happy memories from my time in hospital, mainly about the art classes they had. The fear of relapsing still preys on my mind so I am on a lot of medication.

Trying my best to get to my groups, I have Pavestones where I do Art on Monday and Hand Embroidery on Thursday. I also attend a Reading Group, face-to-face Writing Group, a Zoom writing group and sometimes a Sewing Group. Despite it getting more difficult to go to them, when I do, I find fulfilment in them. Without my Groups I would be more depressed: they've given me a sense of purpose and meaning to my life.

I would love to go back to university but had to leave my Fine Art degree because of my health and my mum's passing. Wanting to study Fashion and Textiles, at the moment the travel and studio work would be just too much for me, even part time. So, at the moment I watch videos about fashion on YouTube and dream about going to Central Saint Martin's where my hero Alexander McQueen studied. I know it's a pipe dream, but it inspires me to keep up my interest in fashion.

Fashion, art, writing, are the three main areas of my Creativity. I find it hard to be creative at the moment with all my health problems, but I will keep trying because that is what I live for. When I'm creative I'm happier, achieving something. Without my creativity I would be lost. It makes me who I am.

I'd love to make people more aware of my *Invisible Illnesses* because I feel alone and know others feel the same. I once tried to set up an IBS support group, but I ended up being used as a babysitter and the members stopped coming. It's not exactly something one can talk about in the open which is a shame. No one in the street would ever know about my invisible illnesses. I'm trying a new approach using meditations on YouTube. I don't think it's working but will keep at it as the doctors can't help me, so I'm left to my own devices.

I always try to inspire others which is why I wrote this piece. I want to be a voice for those who suffer in silence.

You are not alone.

Keep believing in life.

Just keep going.

We can get through this together.

Noreen Kane

Being a Belfast woman who has been uprooted and replanted several times in different countries and continents, has made Noreen Kane a little peculiar. Having performed poorly at school under the loving tutelage of the nuns, she found herself at 30 yrs old avidly studying in a foreign country to become an Occupational Therapist and now at 69 yrs old doing an Open University degree in Arts & Humanities and Creative Writing. With a short span of attention and all the traits of a Scorpio, she is consistently sucking the marrow out of life. After writing alone for 65 yrs, she became a member of two Northern Irish Writing Groups, *Words Inc* and *this writing thing*, 2024. She has discovered that she relishes critique, as it has improved her writing and performing skills. Her writing isn't specific to one genre, but the more intense the emotion the better. Noreen's ambition is to wake up breathing.

being human

lovers of leavers deserve a slow goodbye

no hesitant peel away nor tentative retreat

there is no perfect immaculate moment

present implacable facts   allow to marinate

Leaver has had time

dithering in doubt

bolstering through broken hopes

submerged in sadness they reached this junction

joy shredded by resentment

optimism doused by indifference

they are desperate for change

Lover wallows complacently   unaware of the seismic shifts

never reacting well to security being ripped out of their throat

I didn't ask for this...

laziness did

I didn't break us up...

neglect did

it's not my fault...

it 50% is

I don't want you to go...

*but **I** do*

time to grieve

Leaver accords patience while yearning to be selfish

firmness when they want to bend

strength when battle-weary and craving rest

consistency when they long to be compassionate

why?

because they want to be a Leaver more than a Lover

but more than that they want to be human

Her very Irish ending

Dreamy ribbons of whispery mist hung over the lake. Hurled in an arc by a muscular arm, the ashes hung as if suspended by the fog. The company watched it swirl in the breeze and approach them. Transfixed they stood with mouths hanging. Then it drifted to the water.

I swear I can taste it on my lips

A huff of laughter started low. Then a snort and soon the communal humour lifted in the air.

They knew. They remembered the degree of devilry.

It was probably a nipple or a varicose vein,

according to whom she wanted to provoke.

She didn't need to be present; they carried her inside.

They knew her.

to be continued

cat sat on a mat   he'd smelled the rat
woman on a mat   body flat
sprawled prone on the floor just as he had left her
feline licking   she felt better

swish-a-la-wish and there came the knock
the whingeing   the whining   the tick of a tock
pitiful promises   regret for the pain
all heard before   all said in vain

hours came and went   'twas no longer light
lying there   s l o w l y   she bled out all fight
relationships awry   men gone wrong
was it her   was it them   what a swan song

telephone ringing   cat yawned at her
purring he curled up on her sweater
silence prevailed   she felt weak
closing her eyes   longing for sleep

drifting away she felt no cold
yearned for peace   felt so damned old
the pool of blood   ignored by them both
slid over the floor like a lazy sloth

the cat remained with his departed friend
several days went by   he stayed to defend
his carer   his petter   his feeder   his mate
another would claim him

. . . he just had to wait

ferocious daughters

throaty wolf wails filled the rain-damp garden

she was going for the ugly cry

no restraint on these emotions

unable to stay where i was concealed

i bridged the chasm between us

wading through cold treacle towards her

holding my arms open like a crucified icon

slotting like spoons into our places

bending her long slender body to fit around my pudding belly

her collar-bone prodding my cheek

holding me tight she squeezed the breath from my lungs like a cheap balloon

chest driven guttural sounds now echoed in my ear.

I can't do this anymore Mammy

So don't   just don't do it anymore

smoothing her spine i stroked a finger over the nape of her neck

her damp red tendrils sticking to my face like sweat

gentling slowly like a horse, as if given permission to calm, she didn't rise yet

rooted in place i knew i would never be the first to let go

Witness

there's glory in a single moment of life

protested the dead baby

a sucking of air

    inflation of lungs

        then gone

but for that golden spark   that sizzle of life

that neuron of being

I was

because I was, I always will

in a thought

    a memory

        an anniversary

we were witness to us

you keep my moment alive

Kirsty Mowat

Born and bred in the city of Belfast, after many years of travelling Kirsty Mowat now lives on the north coast of Northern Ireland. Lover of languages, she worked as a translator before moving into the proofreading and editing scene. Recently reigniting her passion for creative writing, Kirsty attends *Words Inc* Writers' Group in Coleraine. Other than school magazine pieces and caption competition entries, this is her first publication. When not reading or writing, Kirsty enjoys motorbiking, hang-gliding and staring at the sea.

Handheld Addiction

Necks angled towards the ground
blinkered bodies bumble
oblivious to the world.

Eyes cast down
sight line perpendicular
to a cradling hand.
An invisible bond.

Digits grip a rectangular shell
a life-giving energy.
Thumb tapping touchscreen
the message that must be sent.

The promise of the latest news

who was where

and why and when.

Instant camera captures

moments otherwise missed.

In the other hand

a plastic-coated source of scented wakes:

watermelon strawberry vanilla.

Electronic equilibrium

analogous noxious nicotine.

Facecloth

That song, that song.

Whisking me back twenty years. When they were all still alive. When life was good.

Don't think. Don't think.

Eyes wide, I will the tears to stay away.

Quick. Think of something else.

But two lacrimal lines run parallel to my nose, hesitating as they reach the corners of my mouth.

No, this isn't the wind in my face. No sting from chopped onions. No irritant eyelash. No. No excuses. Admit these tears of sadness. From the depths to tear ducts which can contain them no longer. Emotions marked by damp, vertical runways.

What antidote?

A simple square of cotton – soaked, squeezed, steaming – soothing my eyes, nose and mouth. An underestimated healing touch. A welcome dampness on the face.

I inhale. My muscles relax. All is well.

Belfast Bound

I'm nearly there. Back in the city where I began. Before a quarter-century of travel. To places long-haul days away – or just one and a half hours by train. How can they seem so equally foreign? Is distance no factor in a longing for home?

The sing-song voice interrupts my contemplation: '*Your next stop is …*' (slight pause for the grand reveal) '*Mossley West!*'

This is when I look up, in hungry anticipation. Soon, I am savouring the familiar surroundings: the Cranes, cutting bright sunflower lines across the sky; the mottled blue of the Big Fish; its neighbour, the lady with the hoop, catching the light; the glass-panelled dome of Victoria Square.

The latter landmarks arrived after my maiden departure. As for the nesting, non-migratory Cranes – well, they've *always* been there.

Glazed

Flowers fill the hearse, a patient sentry, parked out front. For the undertaker, a day like any other. For us, this is new, uncharted. Finite.

I look over at Maria, propped up by the marble entrance pillar, numb. Gilt lettering glistens 'Brown & Sons' on the glass doors.

So many times I'd walked past, with a glance inside. Never had I seen myself in there, staring at choices of wood, satin linings, fake gold handles.

***

But that day came – three days ago – when I'd pushed my way in through the glass.

Reception desk.

Showroom.

Dark box-like waiting room.

Closed doors.

I didn't want to be there.

Maria had refused to come. In denial. Needed more time, she said.

'*Yeah, well, so did Mum,*' I'd snapped.

So I was on my own. Meaningless words swirled around me. Branded pen passed to sign on the line. Business completed in a blur.

***

Now, here are the floral arrangements I must have ordered. Concealing the sickly shining closet below. Mum's request for carboard, ignored. '*It just wouldn't feel right*,' Maria had insisted.

I catch Maria's eye. With Herculean effort, she composes herself, manages vertical without the pillar. A nod of acknowledgement. I walk over.

'*Come on, Sis. Let's do this.*'

Linking arms, we walk round the back to Mum's old Clio. A sombre navy colour had seemed more fitting for the occasion than Maria's yellow Mini.

Opening the front passenger door, Maria stoops to get in, exhaling as she sits.

'*Bring it on!*'

Installing myself, I pat the steering wheel, as if to console for the absence of its usual driver.

'*Alright. Let's go.*'

We follow the flower-ridden hearse down the road, polished black and glass gleaming in the light.

Faustina Starrett

The Page Turner

*Inspired by retirement, a new Chapter begins in the book of life. A time of reckoning, recording, harvesting. Turning the page … a new day … making each one count.

Embracing a new chapter after thirty-five years in education and training, Faustina enjoys travel and being a member of reading and writing groups in local libraries. Her creative writing includes prose, poetry and flash fiction. Three of her short bio sketches are included in the book '*Open Space your Place'*, produced by Community Arts Good Relations Project, funded by Northern Ireland Executive, 2023. Faustina is currently enjoying new writing challenges with the writing groups *Words Inc* and *Malvern Writers*, and for *Impspired* publishing house.

Love Legacy

Only a curtain ring
on my finger
worn thin
through loving time

We didn't buy a new one
triggering bloodlines
furore
a wake of childhood memories

Our own vows absorbing
the love and loss of you
a little band of gold
passed on
blessed twice
signalling a new age of loving

Vital as air
worn lightly

down

the

years

Stilettos

- Prompt exercise : She always avoided me like the plague after that ~

Stiletto points on the shiny tiles. Click, click, the precision of a heartbeat. The sound speeds up to a staccato pulse as I approach the exit. She lunges forward catching my scarf. I feel her anxiety in the tug.

Please wait, Hazel, I need you to hear me out.

I stop, turn to face her gaze head on, hold it.

> *I've been too ashamed to face you, Hazel. I presented your Pitch as mine when you'd put so much work into it. Without that commission I was a goner. I'd convinced myself it was ok. You were safe, you've plenty of work in the pipeline. It's yours to Project Manage if you still want it. I'm so sorry I did such an underhand thing.'*

I can see she's sorry. Her distance hurt me more than the deceit. She is better than me at Pitches, I'd missed our teamwork. My trust had been bruised. Still, we'd bagged the client, and she'd offered me back what I do best. I played it straight.

I'll think about your offer, Alex. Catch up with you at International Women's day. Maybe we can get a coffee after the Launch.

Out the exit, into the cold winter sunshine, a deep breath exhaling a quiet joyful relief, leaving it all behind.

It is Friday.

Riptide (on Mullaghderg)

Panoramic views on all sides

Atlantic Ocean sweeping in

Out there the sea goes on forever

rolls in here on tidal rhythms

Sea goes out ... sea comes in ...

Familiar soundscape

The pull and drag of waves on the shore

Hypnotic call to unsuspecting water babies

Serrated wave-edges coming at them sideways

Contours powered from below

seduced by skies blue and black

sedated by familiar echoes on repeat

Sea goes out ... the sea comes in ....

Moving below the waterline into perfect alignment

lifted in a clean sweep

demonic energies from the oceans volcanic pit

Out ... Out ... defying gravity

faster than the speed of sound

feathers far flung to where the sea goes on forever

Sea goes out ... sea comes in ...

On the beach

lonely clothes wait

A tide goes out ... a tide comes in

Mary Farrell : Editor

Mary Farrell

designed by Steve Cawte

Mary Farrell co-ordinates three weekly writing Groups *Sanderlings*, *Words Inc* and *Write So!,* is a regular guest Facilitator for *Portglenone Writers*, and each month attends *this writing thing* in Derry. Previously a member of The UK Chartered Institute of Editing and Proofreading, she is now in her third year as a member of the Reedsy Publishing Company Judging Panel for their weekly competition. Since January 2025, she is also a Professional Member of the Irish Writers Society, based in Dublin.

Her published work includes a trilogy of general Collections, *It's like Walking a Tightrope*, 2021, *Out of the Chrysalis,* 2022 and *A Phoenix Still Rising* in 2023. *Springboards: a Creative Writing Manual for Beginners through to Facilitators* was published in October 2022. The three books in The Circle Trilogy, *The Kingdom, Maybury* and *New Asgarth* were published in 2022, 2023 and 2024. Editor of three other Anthologies, *Irish Hares and Seahorses*, 2022, *Spun Yarns and Woven Words*, 2023, and *Sea Spray and Woodland Glades,* 2024, the books above have all been published by Impspired Press.

She organises two annual Competition/Performance Events *Flash Fiction Portrush* each Spring, and *Impspired Soundwaves* each Autumn, part of the Swell Festival, Portrush.

You can contact Mary at

- www.maryfarrellwriting.com
- email maryfarrell85@hotmail.com
- through her Facebook page.

Rapunzel tresses

Once upon many times...

As prisons go it was better than most. A bedroom, a solar, a tiny room with a cramped wooden tub and seat with a runnel to the outside wall, all three areas fitting compact within the circular space at the top of the tower.

A magnificent view from the window in the solar, her father had announced when he left her there, though he had planned that little could be seen from the slits in other two rooms. In the winter months tapestries absorbed the worst of the damp seeping through from the stone walls, and an inadequate brazier sucked some of the chill from the air.

Persinette hauled up a basket with fresh food every morning and a second each evening with coal and kindling, medicaments and manuscripts, clean clothes and hair combs, all that her father deemed necessary for her to maintain *mens sana in corpore sano.* Rainwater was captured in a wooden tank attached to the outside wall, and during the height of the dry summer when rain was scarce, a third basket holding flagons of water was provided each noontide.

Her father had thought of everything - or at least he prided himself he had - for survival but not comfort.

That way she'd come to her senses, would marry Rupert so that their two kingdoms would be joined for evermore. But the girl was stubborn. It had been three years now; she had turned fifteen. If Rupert had not been so blinded by land-lust and his craving for power, he would have looked elsewhere for a bride long ago.

~ ~ ~

The farm was in the middle of nowhere, on the sunless side of a bleak mountain, fit for only sheep and goats. The two fields in which the potatoes and vegetables were grown, had been clawed from the earth by her grandparents, each grey stone excavated by hand, carried with straining shoulders to the field-edge to build boundary walls.

Her father had grown up there, but not much. He was slight, with a curvature of his shoulders resulting from a malnourished childhood and a lack of Vitamin D. Her mother had come from the Foundling Home in the next valley, left at the door one winter night. She'd been sent to the farm as a worker twelve years from that date, the day of her abandonment designated as her birthday. In time her mother and father married, a logical pragmatic step. As her mother had died giving birth to her, all she knew of her maternal heritage were the few scraps she had been told.

She knew almost as little about her father. After her grandparents left him the farm, a passing-over long before her memory could recall, as she grew the two of them spent their days in silence, with only the most necessary of comments about food, the land, the animals. Once years ago when she spoke, she heard her voice crack from misuse, so she took care now to talk to the sheep, to the potato shoots, to the flames in the fire, and to the strong winds and slight breezes for fear she'd become mute.

The few who visited labelled her strange, but she knew no other way of living. Little did she realise her father intended she never would. Whenever he spoke with others and the subject was raised of her leaving to work elsewhere, or even worse, of her marriage to some local, he'd describe her strangeness, her feyness, her curious ways. Those who heard this would then stay clear, fearing an evil-eyed look or an unexpected curse. He had no intention of being left alone on the farm but knew no second wife could ever be lured here. His few cousins detested the isolation, and the land was too barren to be sold. He was chained to that poor place, and he had decided ... so would she be!

~ ~ ~

Crouched on a stool at the rickety table, César could hear his wife snuffling over the plastic basin in the corner. Her tears, falling in steady drops, added little to the two inches of liquid in the bowl. Water was too scarce to waste on washing humans or crockery. The shanty town hut contained nothing as luxurious as a kitchen, just a bench in the corner on which to chop, mash and try to eke out anything edible. Four stones formed an upright rectangle beside it, an insipid fire in their centre, seeping acrid smoke into the already stale air.

On the cross-stone on top, a pot always boiled, on good days with a broth which had colour, on poor ones with a dull insipid brew. On really good days, when he'd found more cans in the rubbish tip than usual and could buy rice or beans, the liquid became a stew. But it was never enough to fill the five of them - he César, his wife, and the children, Eduardo, Maria and baby Carmelita. Three other childish souls had come and gone, pulling faint air into tiny lungs but eating nothing as they fleetingly passed across the family threshold.

The Man was due any minute. César turned over the same arguments in his head which he had kneaded many times before. Indeed, he had thought of little else these last weeks. The arrangement was clear. The Man would take Maria. In return, César would get a job in the factory sorting the cans which others like himself would then bring to him. There would be a weekly wage, enough to keep his family alive, enough to rent a different hut further up the hillside where the air was clearer and Eduardo would cough less, where there was a tap which spat out water ... and fewer rats.

He knew of other families who had dealt with the Man, who had in time received letters and photographs proving their little ones were now wives and mothers. The Man was in his own way honourable. He saw his work as charitable, a way for families in the shanty town to survive, and loneliness in distant lands to be eased. César also knew of more lucrative offers from others, but was aware that those girls ended shameful lives with early deaths.

A shape filled the doorway; a shadow etched a pattern on the floor. It was time. César surrendered, as he had known he would, to the inevitable. For the last time he called out, *Maria, come here.*

~ ~

Those of you with half-empty cups will already have written your own endings.

Those of you with half full containers, consider these.

~ ~ ~

Hidden from view, a chivalrous knight had watched the daily proceedings, driven by a noble desire to rescue a prisoner. After many weeks planning, on a certain morning, he knocked out the servant from behind, inserting a long sturdy rope into the basket to be raised. Finding it, she wasted no time in climbing through the solar window and abseiling to the ground. Both were much surprised to see the other, a knight and a young maiden. In the way of such tales, they looked into each other's eyes, married soon after, and lived long and happy lives in a kingdom far away from her father ... and from Rupert.

~ ~ ~

In a world where the only two certainties are death and taxes, even as poor a farm as this one, had an official annual visit, seeking a pittance from a pot which didn't exist. Every May a visitor from the Fiscal Department of Taxation would climb the dreary path to the farm half-door. She was just in from the hillside, with her bare brown feet, her cheeks rose-blown by the freshest of air, and her hair wild and free, garlanded with fresh picked daisies. This first sighting, the newly appointed young Clerk told their grandchildren, he would never forget until the day the clay covered him.

~ ~ ~

The letter had been read out to them so many times the paper was now as fragile as ancient lace, but her words, dictated to a scribe in Mesquite, near Dallas, had long since been memorised.

He calls me his sinta Papa. He's been learning Tagalog so that the baby and I remember who we are and where we came from. He loves us both so much. I live in a fine house with two bedrooms, a slate roof, and such a grand kitchen! We even have a car. I called the baby César. I think he looks like you.

And indeed, no matter how often the family looked at the three photographs, that fact was clear. His daughter grinned at the camera with her mother's eyes, but everyone agreed that his Texan grandson looked exactly like him.

C'mon, you don't believe

fairy-tale endings are possible.

Printed in Great Britain
by Amazon

62946714R00268